NEW

S0-ABT-942

PRAYERS FOR THE DEAD

PRAYERS
FOR THE DEAD

STORIES BY
DENNIS VANNATTA

WHITE PINE PRESS • FREDONIA, NY

©1994 Dennis Vannatta

All rights reserved. This book, or parts thererof,
may not be reproduced in any form without permission.

This is a work of fiction.
Any resemblence to characters living or dead
is purely coincidental.

Acknowledgments:
"The Summer Fair" and "The Man Who Came to Love the Heat" were
originally published in *Wind*; "Kohlrabi" and "Old Soldier"in *Ellipsis*;
"Wesley Tucker's 'Misterious Indïan Burial Grounds'" in *Prairie
Winds*; "Them Bones" and "Passover" in *South Dakota Review*.

Publication of this book was made possible,
in part, by grants from
the National Endowment for the Arts
and the New York State Council on the Arts.

Book design by Elaine LaMattina

Cover painting: "The Old Flour Mill"
by Thelma Winter, Eden, New York

Printed in the United States of America

9 8 7 6 5 4 3 2 1

ISBN 1-877727-39-3

WHITE PINE PRESS
10 Village Square
Fredonia, New York 14063

PRAYERS FOR THE DEAD

for my mother

Contents

PRAYERS FOR THE DEAD

THE PLAIN

1.

"IT WAS A CLEAR BRIGHT SUNDAY morning, and you could smell the wild roses in the air as we rode along Rosebud Creek," George Workman would always begin.

Years later, after his father's death, John Workman would sit out on the porch of the little store, watching the miners below him, black with coal dust, trail home. And he would find himself repeating his father's story, but softly, so that Lelia, just inside, wouldn't hear.

"We broke up a couple of miles off the Little Bighorn," John whispered, lips barely moving. The miners walked slowly down the road along the base of the hill. As they passed the trail that led up to the store, occasionally one would pause and look up. It was a good walk up the trail, and even if somebody decided to come up, John would have time to finish his story.

"Benteen wandered off to the south and west with D, H, and K—heaven knows what for—and Custer took his five companies north along the ridge."

Lelia could never understand why the store had to be up on the hill. Tired miners don't want to make that climb up the trail, she would say. Move the store down on the road, she would say, and we'll make us some money. Better yet, move on into town and we'll make money hand over fist.

And she was right, of course. Lelia had a head on her shoulders. "The store's here on the hill because that's where my daddy put it," he'd tell her over and over, but that wasn't good enough for her. She just didn't understand history. None of them understood history, and that's why his daddy had told his story and kept telling it until the day he died.

"I don't even remember when was the last time I saw Custer. About the time his column would have been moving out of sight, us in Reno's column was coming up on the creek, and by then we could see the big village. Sweet Jesus, it just seemed to go on forever. This old boy next to me, Thompson I believe it was, lets his big old clabber-footed horse splash all over me going across the creek, and I says, 'Hell, boy, don't drown me afore I get kilt!' We knew we were goners right from the start, you see. The night before, the Rees and Crow scouts had been singing their death songs. Anyway, we barreled on ahead, and of course it's the Unkpapas we run into. I'd a rather it'd been any of them except the Unkpapas. So they come for us, them and the Santees, whooping and blowing on them bone whistles, and Reno right off has us dismount and form a skirmish line, which we stay in all of about ten seconds, and then we take off. We head for the trees and stay there awhile, but them Unkpapas are coming right in with us, chopping us up, so we take off for the creek, the hill just the other side. Call it Reno's Hill today, what I'm told. Anyway, my horse had done been shot out from under me, and I just hot-footed it, ran through the brush and weeds along the creek, across the creek, and up that Christy-long ravine up to the top of the hill where we sat waitin' three days for General Terry to come, two days with Sioux all around us, sun boiling our brains, men going crazy with the thirst, dead horses bloating up and stinking like Satan's outhouse..."

John's voice rose as he got on into the story, always did—he couldn't help it. Then he remembered Lelia and stopped, craned around to peer through the door. He couldn't see Lelia, but he heard her back in the storeroom working. John couldn't figure out how she could find so much to do, and she couldn't figure out how he could avoid finding it, apparently, because she was always after him. Build me an extra bin for dried beans, she'd say one day. Build on an extra room and we can stock some hardware, she'd be after him the next. If you don't want to work around here, she'd say, get you a job down in the mine. I can handle the store alone.

His daddy would roll over in his grave if John took a job digging coal. Didn't she understand that? That was why he'd gone off into the army with Annie pregnant with John. Gold had been discovered in the Black Hills, and if things looked right when he got out west, he'd take his discharge out the back door and pan for gold. If not, he'd come back from the army with enough saved up to open a general store. George Workman's sons weren't going to cough their lives away in a hole in the ground. And lo and behold, he had come back with the money, and with his story besides.

". . . and I loved that hill, sun and stink and all. I hugged that hill like I'd hug my momma. Up there we could see what they done to the ones that got caught on the plain, sticking stuff in their eyes, hacking off their privates, chopping their legs and arms and heads clean off. I was happy to be on that hill, I'll tell you, instead of down on the plain all out in the open where they could see you for miles and miles, no place to hide."

So when he came home, George built the house on the hill and then the little store next to it, and he'd tell his story over and over and over, but it didn't do any good.

Reno George they'd call him behind his back, or Yellow George. And sometimes to his face if they'd drunk a bit too much. "Custer dead a hero and Yellow George sits on his hill in Pennsylvania." George wouldn't get mad, just exasperated that they couldn't seem to understand. How hot it was. How many Sioux there'd been. How they'd hollererd and blown those whistles! Custer? How could they've gone to Custer's aid if they didn't know where he was, didn't know he was in trouble? Hell, man, they'd cussed Custer for three days because he didn't come to *their* rescue. They didn't know, they just didn't know. When General Terry finally arrived and they went to that dusty ridge a few miles north to see, at first they didn't understand what they were looking at. George thought it was a field full of white boulders, boulders with feathers sticking out of them. They'd counted thirty-six arrows in what was left of John Doogan, who George had dropped knives with not a week before.

They just couldn't be made to understand, not

even Annie, who must have heard the story a thousand
times. Annie'd never say anything when George told his
story, nor when he tacked up the William Cary illustra-
tion from the *Daily Graphic* on the store wall and would
collar one of the rare customers and explain,

"Now that ain't the Custer I knew, no sir. You
wouldn't believe long flowing locks on him at the Little
Bighorn, not if you knew how hot Montana could get in
June."

But if she didn't understand, only once in his life
could John recall his mother making anything like a com-
plaint to George, and that was when George decided to
take his family into Pittsburgh to see the big Mulvany
canvas of the Last Stand. The trip was sixty-five miles,
four days there and back, and took all the money Annie
had saved up for a store-bought dress to bury herself in.

"Oh George, oh George," was all she'd said before
throwing her apron up over her face and turning to the
wall.

George died in 1892, a year after Annie, almost
two years after the trip to Pittsburgh, and John married
Lelia in 1893. Lelia had grown up dirt poor, an Armstrong
from over on Granite Ridge, and she thought any man
who owned a store was rich—or could be if he'd only be
smart and move it down to where the people were.

It was only then, when she started in on that a few
months after they were married, that John told her his
father's story. But she didn't understand. She hadn't heard
George tell it himself, of course, and she hadn't been
there on the plain or on the hill, hadn't been there, even,
when John was growing up and the children would circle
round him whooping and shouting, "Little Reno, Little

Reno, Yellow John, Yellow John!" She *wouldn't* understand, not even after John told her the story a hundred times. (And once, when she'd heard those first words coming—"It was a bright clear Sunday morning, and you could smell the wild roses . . ."—she clasped her hands over his mouth and said, "Dammit John!"—the only time she ever cussed, a footwashing Baptist.)

So now, when the need to tell the story came upon him, John would go outside and whisper the words to the hill because he was afraid of Lelia and her temper, feared her almost as much as he loved her.

*

They had begun to think that they were fated to remain childless, but Mary came in the bitter February of 1899. On New Year's Eve of that same year Lelia took John's hand and placed it firmly on her belly, held it there.

"Another one coming, John. This one a boy," she said. "Know what I'm gonna call him? Yellow George. I'll whisper 'Yellow George' while I'm nursing him. Leastways that way it won't be no surprise when the other kids call him that. Then you can tell him your story, and you and him can sit on this hill forever talking about all you're afraid of. Coward."

John staggered out of the house and sat down in the snow, stared up into the black sky.

"You're right about everything," he said when he came back in. His eyes were blinded by tears of repentence, voice choked with joy and love. "I won't nail my son to a dusty hill I ain't never seen, what I done to myself. I'll give him a life in the new century. Sweetheart, we're gonna move to Garden City, Kansas."

It was Lelia's turn to be stunned. She'd hoped to move to the bottom of the hill, not to Kansas. It was where her brother Ike had gone two years before. At Christmas they'd received a postcard from him that had said, "Hi! Everythings grate in Garden City! Come on out! Make your fortion!"

The bottom of the hill, that's all she'd hoped for. John tried to explain to her that Kansas was the plains— what his daddy had always taught him to fear—and now he was going to face up to that fear, free himself from that hilltop, and give his son to the twentieth century. "Kansas is Kiowa country," was the last thing he'd said, but she wasn't listening. She felt like she'd walked down a long flight of stairs in the dark, thought she was at the bottom, then stepped off into a headlong fall. Before she'd recovered all the way from the shock, John had sold the house, store, and land, and that spring she found herself in Pittsburgh, boarding the train, heading west.

2.

Many years later it would be said that Sunday's Hollow got its name from the Reverand Billy Sunday, who preached there one day in the 1920s, or maybe the 1930s. The only problem with this account was that it could not possibly have been true. Billy Sunday had never been within a hundred miles of that out-of-the-way corner of the Missouri Ozarks, and besides, it was already called Sunday's Hollow when the Workmans rode their wagon down into it in June, 1900.

Some of the residents of the Hollow claimed to remember—or claimed to remember their parents remembering—an old Scotsman named Thomas Sunday who had owned a good deal of the Hollow at one time, bought it from the Osages, most of whom then moved on west.

Sunday's Hollow was a little valley cut by the Grand North creek as it ran generally west. The Hollow began a few miles west of Warsaw, then ended after ten miles or so. When you climbed up out of it you'd be in Jerico, a scant collection of shacks with a tiny store on the west end.

Sunday's Hollow was out of the way from everywhere, and the land was more rock than soil. John Workman could hardly say how he'd managed to bring his family into it. A man had gotten on the train at Olney, Illinois, and by the time they'd pulled into St. Louis, he'd convinced John to cash in his tickets and put the money in on a wagon and team of horses. "You'll need them when you get to Kansas and start your own farm. Can't farm without them. Every penny you spend on this train is one penny wasted. Buy yourself that team and wagon, and there's your transportation to Kansas, and man's best friend on the farm, too!"

John'd spent almost all their money on the wagon and team, so when they finally made it to Jefferson City after a week and another friendly stranger advised them to take the Adkins Road south and save the fifty cent ferry fee across the Missouri, it seemed like a good idea.

"When the Adkins Road runs out, you just start angling off to the south and west. Follow the sun, and before you know it you'll be in Kansas."

The hills were as high and steep as the ones they'd left in Pennsylvania, the roads generally no more than rough trails, and the woods dense with underbrush. By the time they reached Sunday's Hollow, Mary had been crying for most of the last two days, and Lelia sat silent and grim as an idol.

They came up out of the Hollow at around noon and stopped at the Jerico store, bought hoop cheese and crackers for their dinner. A huge, slow-moving woman with a tired, gentle face came over to Lelia and put her hand on her arm.

"Don't you worry, hon, the way'll be easier here on. You're out of the hills now."

A mile west of Jerico they crested a gentle rise, broke out of a stand of hickory trees, and saw stretched before them, mile on mile, the plain.

*

Lelia did not cry when John—after staring ahead of him for the longest time—hauled the wagon around and headed back to Jerico. She did not begin to cry until he had gone into the store, but once she started she cried hard, pulling her bonnet down over her face as she held Mary on her lap. When John finally got back, he could not console her. She would only point to the sign above the door and weep. When he did not understand, she finally sobbed in frustration,

"The sign, the sign, John! Don't you see? They ain't spelled it right. They'd've spelled it right in Pennsylvania, John. Oh John, where are we?"

"We're home," he said.

She stopped crying then, sat silent on the long ride back into the Hollow, and didn't begin to cry again until John pulled up before the tiny log house. John knew why she was crying then because she managed to get out one word: "clapboard." And for a moment he too thought wistfully of the clapboard house atop the hill in Pennsylvania and wondered at a log cabin, mud-chinked and windowless, in the twentieth century.

But then of course it wasn't the twentieth century. That was another thing he'd learned from the man on the train—1900 was the last year of the old century, not the first of the new. The man had explained the arithmetic of it, which John couldn't follow but figured must be right. John hadn't told Lelia about it, sensing that she wasn't ready for one more blow.

John finally coaxed Lelia off the wagon—almost carried her really—and into the cabin where she sat and cried and nearly broke his heart when she sobbed, "John, John, oh John, I don't want to be poor people." And he didn't know what to say.

John went back outside when the man with the greasy black hair caught in a knot at the back of his head and then flowing halfway down his back rode up on a mule, a long-legged boy behind him. The man got down and talked to John for a while outside. Then the boy rode off on the mule, and the man climbed onto their wagon and started off. That's when Lelia stopped crying—when she realized there wasn't any use in it.

John came back in. His face was almost white, and his lips were trembling. He sat down at the rough-hewn, hickory table stained with grease and tobacco juice and ran a hand through his hair.

"Nice enough fellow," he said. "Mockingbird Carter, he calls himself. Osage."

He thought that Lelia would begin to cry again, but she didn't. Something hard had come into her face that he couldn't bear to look at, so he got up and walked outside.

Nothing had gone the way he'd planned. He had blundered at every step, and now he had led them into something they'd never escape from.

He wandered off up the road until he realized that he was going in the direction that the Indian had taken. Then he stopped, and felt his breath come in rapid jerks and a cold sweat spring to his face.

For the first time since he left the hill in Pennsylvania, he began to recite his father's story, but he had whispered only the first sentence when he remembered Lelia back in the cabin. He turned to head back but paused when, from a little clearing to his right, he caught the sweet scent of spring flowers.

*

John stood before the table. Lelia sat, staring at the wall. He knew that he might have to stand there a long time, but eventually she would have to turn back to him, and then he would offer her the wild roses.

THE SUMMER FAIR

ELLY PAUSED IN THE HENHOUSE to breathe in the rich odor of straw, meal, chickens, and eggs. She usually didn't waste time thinking about it—gathering eggs was just a chore to her, after all. But at the Wednesday night prayer meeting Reverand Greene had told some long-winded tale about eggs and hens and roosters, and afterward her older brother George had nodded wisely and said, "Yes, eggs is life."

"No," Elly murmured to the hens lined up on their nests, eyeing her nervously, "eggs, is money."

Elly saved all that she made from the eggs of her four hens—Gertie and Betty and Queenie and Red—just as Mary and Viola did. Elly's momma kept the three canning jars filled with pennies and nickels up behind the stove. They weren't marked, but the three sisters knew whose was whose. George didn't sell eggs for money because he was a man, and a man could cut wood to haul into Warsaw or work for a neighbor during harvest and haying time.

They all spent their money on different things: George mostly on shells for his rifle and Mary on ribbons for her hair because she was getting to be a young woman now and Viola on Horehound candy at the store in Jerico. Elly, though, was going to spend every cent she had at the annual Sunday's Hollow Summer Fair.

Elly moved to the dark end of the hen house and slid her hand carefully under Red—who ruffled her feathers and swung her terrified eye around in jerks—and eased out the egg, then turned and danced out of the hen house. In the yard she paused a moment and looked around for Kaiser Bill, but she didn't see him. Kaiser Bill was a mean rooster. He could run as fast as a dog and would peck off your toes.

Elly tore across the yard and jumped up on the porch. Kaiser Bill was nowhere to be seen. Some day she'd knock that rooster's head off with a hoe handle. The screen door slapped shut behind her, and she strutted into the kitchen where her momma was cooking bacon and eggs for breakfast. Elly sat down at the table and looked at her mother's back, bent over the iron stove. Elly held an egg close to her nose, and even with coffee and bacon strong in the air, she could still smell its warm, delicate scent. Chicks were in there. If you didn't eat the eggs, chicks would grow in there. That was life, George said. But if she brained Kaiser Bill, there wouldn't be any eggs. She usually didn't think about it much, but today was the day of the Summer Fair, a special day, and she thought about special things.

"Here, Elly."

Her momma waved her over to the stove without

turning.

Elly walked over with the basket, and her momma's hand reached down and took two eggs and cracked them one at a time. When they hit the hot skillet where the bacon had been frying, the eggs sent up a hiss and a different kind of smell.

2.

Mary sat on the side of the bed and gazed at her image in the mirror. Through the thin wall she heard the men tramp into the kitchen, laughing loudly. Daddy and George had done their chores, and they would eat breakfast now.

"Breakfast, girls!"

Chairs scraped across the floor in the next room as the men sat down. The screen door banged shut, and either Viola or Elly skipped across the floor to the table. Mary could smell the coffee and eggs, but she wasn't hungry. Breakfast had a man smell to it. She stared dreamily at herself in the mirror, then stood up and inspected her dress. She ran her fingers lightly down her dress from her shoulders across her breasts to her thighs. Momma had made it for her Easter, but she had worn it only three times since, so it was like new. A blue the color of a robin's egg.

"Mary, you come and eat!" Elly had popped her head into the room and scrambled back to the table before Mary turned from the mirror.

She sighed and strolled on into the kitchen and took her glass of milk and a strip of bacon from the plate, but she didn't sit down. Careful not to wrinkle her dress, she leaned back against the pie safe, took a sip of the milk, and raised the bacon to her lips. But she had no appetite, so she sat the bacon back down on the plate.

"You eat your bacon," her mother called over from the stove, where she was now dunking chicken parts in flour and laying them in the hot skillet.

"I'm not hungry, Momma."

Her mother walked over and took her plate and slid half the food off onto George's plate and the other half onto her father's. George put two slices of bacon into his mouth at once.

"I bet she'd eat if Kuuurt Schneiiiiiider was here to hold her haaand!" drawled Elly, rolling her eyes as George and Viola guffawed.

Elly jumped up out of her chair and stood poised to sprint for the door, but Mary didn't move. She couldn't be bothered with children. She watched George sop up the last bit of egg yellow with a crust of bread and wash it down with a gulp of black coffee.

George was only sixteen, yet everyone called him a man. He was nearly a head taller than Kurt Schneider, but Kurt was two years older, so he was a man too. There was no question of that. He would buy her pie at the auction, she was sure of that. She sauntered over to the blushing hot stove and played with her finger around the egg-white topping piled high like sun-scorched clouds over the chocolate filling.

"Is it a good one, Momma?"

"Will be if you don't go and spoil it."

Her mother sat down for a moment at the table and gulped down two forkfuls of scrambled eggs, took a sip of coffee, let another spoonful of sugar fall into it, rubbed her hair away from her face, sat back slowly and wearily in the chair, and sighed. Then she shot up, abandoning the coffee and eggs, and strode over to the stove, shooed Mary back and stabbed at the chicken sizzling and popping in the skillet.

"Oh dear, dearie me, I do so hope my chocolate pie is a good one, I do so want my Kurtie pie to love my chocolate pie, oh dearie me," crooned Elly as she floated around the kitchen, batting her eyelids and extending her arms like a robin curling on the lip of a breeze.

George sat his cup down and put his hand over his mouth, trying to supress a laugh. Viola screamed and pounded the table and pointed at Mary and sing-songed, "Kurt and Mary sittin' in a tree, K-I-S-S-I-N-G. How many kisses did she receive?"

"Enough now," father said quietly. Elly tore out the front door. Viola paid strict attention to her plate, and George smiled and shook his head.

Mary wasn't even angry. Elly was such a baby anyway. She knew nothing of men or the way a woman could feel for a man. Her father had silenced them all with two words, two words and the quiet strength of his manhood, like an odor in the room. There was nothing that a woman would not do for such a man. One day she would find hers, and when she did she would follow him to the ends of time, and they would become one in the forge of their tender, fierce love.

3.

"You grab ahold of some sawgrass and you'll wish you hadn't," warned George, but Elly just looked over and stuck her tongue out at him and went on grabbing at weeds and leaves of trees that rolled by the wagon as they rumbled down the road toward the field where the Summer Fair was held each year. The Turnbulls and their matched pair were behind them, and Elly would strip a handful of leaves from a branch that ventured too close and fling it back at the big, snorting stallions.

The road was too narrow for the Turnbulls to pass, so they just laid back, but single riders, young men of the Hollow and nearby Jerico, rode by when the road opened up occasionally. Elly became bored with throwing leaves at the oblivious Turnbull horses, so she sat back in the rear corner of the wagon—with George in the other corner opposite and Mary and Viola in the front of the bed, facing them—and contented herself with staring at the scenery and shouting at the young men as they rode past.

Just as the road slumped down to the creek that bordered the field where the tents and booths and tables of the Summer Fair lay spread, Norton Awtrey passed them. Norton was to go to college in St. Louis, some said, and it was rumored that he had his eye on an automobile. If that weren't enough, today he wore a *uniform*, stiff and heavy and deep brown with bright gold buttons and black boots that glistened out of the stirrups as he rode in the sun, and as he went past he turned slightly and touched his hand to the corner of his hat. They all waved and shouted.

Mary sat twisted around in the wagon gazing off

after him as he rode over to where the other young men were congregated around their horses. Elly sprang up to the front beside Mary to deliver some appropriate taunt, but she hesitated when she heard her momma say, "There'll be some killed before this is done. There'll be a lot of boys killed."

Elly stuck her head up between her momma's and daddy's shoulders and said, "What're you talking about, Momma? We ain't in no war, are we? The United States of America ain't fighting no Germans, are we Daddy?"

"Well," her daddy shrugged as he eased the wagon in under the shade of a young elm, "not yet anyhow."

Her momma turned and shot a sad glance at George as he scrambled down out of the back of the wagon. Elly looked at George with his black hair flopping in the breeze and his gangling but strong arms and shoulders stretching the clean starched shirt and overalls every which way, and it was so funny to think of George dying or any of the young men dying that Elly fell to the bed of the wagon, kicked her heels in the air and laughed.

4.

Mary lowered the chicken breast again as another young man galloped by on his horse. He cut off of the road and across the clearing to where the others were standing in groups between horses tethered to the trees that ringed the field. He rode with head low next to the horse's neck, raised slightly out of the saddle, and as he neared the knot of horses and young men, he leaned back and bounced the horse to a halt, its legs rammed straight into the ground like fence posts, and at the same instant he flew out of the saddle and landed in a run that brought him with a laugh to the midst of his back-slapping companions.

"You going to eat that white meat, Mary?"

She looked down at the chicken breast in her hand, then passed it over to George.

"I guess I'm not hungry right now," she said.

Kurt Schneider was somewhere in the group of young men. She had seen him ride by on his daddy's horse.

"You're going to eat something, Mary Workman," her mother said as she shoved the plate of fried chicken at Mary.

Florence Oates was crossing over toward them from across the road where the Workmans had their picnic spread. Her father got up and headed off toward the produce exhibits where the other men were beginning to gather. Mary stood up and brushed at the back of her dress to make sure no bits of grass clung there.

"I guess I don't want anything else, Momma," she said.

"Oh well, go on then," her mother sighed. "You make me tired with all your moonin' anyway."

Mary joined Florence Oates, and the two ambled over toward the tents and booths. They walked wide around the freak show, where a man with a cane was exhorting all to pay their one thin dime to see the fire-breathing woman and the man with the skin of a reptile. They strolled through the tent that housed the cakes and pies and jams and preserves for the cooking contest. Mary thought of her chocolate pie, which wasn't for the contest—it was for the auction. She hoped it was good. At one of the nickel booths they watched little Johnny Ridgeway spin the arrow and win a wooden soldier— black and red with a red feather as a plume for its hat. And at the merry-go-round they watched and laughed and pointed as Elly rode a high-prancing stallion round and up and down, up and down.

Florence was excited, chattering constantly. Had Mary seen Norton Awtrey in his army uniform? The United States wasn't at war but would be soon, Florence had heard Norton say, and other men too. It was all the men talked of. It was only a matter of time, and Norton might as well get in early and make hay.

They walked over toward the produce and live-stock exhibits where the men were gathered in knots of four and five around the tilted boxes of yellow and white field corn and oats, milo, timothy, alphalpha, the tables laden with boxes of tomatos, cucumber, squash, okra, green beans, apples, and pears. Farther on were tempo-rary pens set up for swine, sheep, and cattle; in the mid-dle was a larger, sturdier pen where stomped, with slow and powerful majesty, a black angus bull.

Florence pointed out Norton Awtrey standing with a group of men by the livestock exhibits. Mary looked across the road where the other young men Norton's age were cavorting around the horses. One rode away from the group at a gallop, then after a short dis-tance freed his feet from the stirrups and leaned far back in the saddle, his hands extended behind him and his legs pressed tight into the horse's neck. Suddenly, the horse swerved and the boy scrambled up into the saddle and lunged for the reins, almost falling off. The other boys whooped and shouted and Florence giggled, but Mary didn't think it was so funny.

Mary and Florence walked between the rows of tilted boxes of field corn. It would be another hour before the pie sale. Mary saw her mother wandering among the produce a few yards away, but most of the other women were with their children at the game booths or were gathering in the tent for the baking judging. Across the row of boxes, a small group of men were laughing and spitting tobacco juice on the straw-littered ground. She saw her father and George farther off, where the horseshoe pitch was.

One of the men across from them stopped laughing long enough to say, "You know that Lois didn't mean nothing by it. Arthur just needed a partner and she was the closest woman around, so she just said, 'Oh sure, I'll dance.' Then I go outside and there's Bracey Pimm sitting on the step. 'Oh boo hoo hoo!' he says. 'Oh boo hoo hoo! I loved her so and now she's gone!'"

The man choked with laughter, and the others wiped tears of laughter out of their eyes with hard, red knuckles and spat tobacco juice on the ground.

"'I loved her so and now she's gone', he says," squealed the man again, screwing up his mouth trying to imitate Bracey Pimm's harelipped speech.

A boy ran over from across the road.

"A race is on!" he hollered. "Kurt Schneider bet Billy Lewis three dollars that that mare of his dad's will beat Billy's quarter horse from here to the school and back!"

He ran on to another group and repeated the news, then on to another. The group of men glanced across the road to where the boys were gathered around the horses, then returned to their conversation.

"Reminds me of another story," said the same man. "Ol' Bracey was in Jerico a couple of years ago when the Rineharts was selling out their stables. Remember that? He's looking at these two mares when Rinehart comes up and asks if he's interested in either of them."

The men started to snicker. The speaker screwed up his mouth to imitate the harelip.

"'I want to see the hosses' twat,' says Bracey."

The men squealed and slapped each other on the back. Across the road Kurt Schneider and the Lewis boy were up on their horses, and the others were gathered close. The men at the horseshoe pitch paused occasionally and looked over at them.

"'I want to see the hosses' twat,' says Bracey. You want *what?*' says Rinehart. 'I want to see the hosses' twat,' Bracey says again. So Rinehart, he shrugs and goes over to this old mare and lifts up her tail. 'There it is,' he says. 'No, no no,' says Bracey. 'Twat down the woad! I want to see the hosses twat down the woad!'"

Mary and Florence blushed and moved off quickly. Across the road a shout went up, and the two turned in time to see the riders flinging dust and clods of dirt behind them as they raced off up the road and disappeared into the trees. They walked over toward the horseshoe pits. The games had stoppped for a moment as the men stared off across the road. The riders were out of sight, but they could be faintly heard yet. Then nothing. One of the men took aim and tossed a horseshoe. It bounced off the hard summer ground and rolled several feet past the stake. He raised the other horseshoe, held it delicately poised with his fingertips, and eyed the stake. He had started into his backswing when he paused and turned his head. The riders could be heard again in the distance, a dull drone among the trees. The conversations dropped off. Men sauntered out from behind pens and tables, hands in their pockets and boots scuffling along the ground, peering at the sky and the people around them in seeming unconcern but glancing repeatedly across the road.

In a moment a rider could be distinguished racing up the road through the trees. It was not until he was fully out into the open field and was clearly recognized as Billy Lewis that the second rider, Kurt Schneider, could be seen up the road.

"Lewis won!" someone shouted.

The men turned back to their conversations. The man at the horsehshoe pit lowered the horseshoe, lifted it with a graceful flick of the wrist, and it floated up in a slow, dreamy arc and descended with a plunk around the wooden stake.

5.

Elly pranced out from among the tents and booths, paused, then galloped on to the middle of the road where she reined back, neighed, and kicked at the ground. She looked around, but no one was watching, so she picked up a clod of dirt and hurled it over in the direction of the horses tethered to the trees, where it fell short by a good fifty yards.

She stretched her arms out and soared off across the field toward their wagon, careening across the open ground and catching the back wheel and flying up into the wagon in a single motion. She pulled the blanket off of the basket and removed the jar with the small jangle of coins at the bottom—eyed it in disgust and consternation. Less than half the afternoon gone and already only a few nickels and pennies left. She'd ridden the merry-go-round twice and thrown the darts and spun the prize wheel and drunk a bottle of strawberry sody pop and eaten a caramel apple and probable several other things that she'd forgotten. And more, so much more, that she wanted to do.

She took three nickels and five pennies from the jar, then carefully replaced the lid. She put the coins into her little leather change purse and snapped it shut. Then she spied one surviving chicken wing at the bottom of the basket, drew it out and tore off several cool, salty, slightly charred strips of meat and gulped them down. A tear-eyed mongrel bitch wandered in and out of the edge of trees over toward the wagon. Elly let it get close enough, then fired the remainder of the wing at it. The bitch winced and lurched to the side, then sniffed over to the wing and swallowed it whole.

Elly jumped down from the wagon, clutching the change purse in her fist, and soared off across the field toward the tents and booths. She ran in and out of the droves of people between the exhibits. Watched Arnold Turnbull at the baseball throw and banshee-laughed when he missed the bottles three times in a row. Saw the Indian boy, Robin's Song Carter, spin the prize wheel and went sick with envy when he won a sparkling new, bone-handled pocket knife. Ducked her head under the canvas skirt of the freak show tent and was half-way through when the barker noticed her and chased her out.

Elly spotted Junior Schneider—two years her senior but still in the first grade since he was a little slow—walking behind the sody pop booth. She caught him from behind and spun him down, mashed his face into the ground and twisted his wrist until he screeched, "I got sumpin to tell you! OK? OK? I got sumpin to tell you! OK?"

She let up a little on his wrist, and he told her that Billy Lewis was using the three dollars that he'd won from Junior's older brother, Kurt, to buy a jug of moonshine. Elly had him repeat it several times, and then she flopped on the ground and laughed and laughed. She got up and staggered around, crossing her eyes and letting her tongue hang out of the corner of her mouth, and yelled crazily, "Whee! Gimme some more moonshine! I'm drunk as a skunk!"

She and Junior staggered off through the crowd with crossed eyes and called for moonshine and laughed until their sides ached.

They saw a large group gathered in front of a little raised platform across the way. It was time for the pie sale. They ran past Kurt Schneider sitting glumly under a tree. Junior steered a wide path behind him, but Elly sauntered up close and jeered, "What's the matter, Kurtie boy? Lose all your money?"

Kurt didn't look up.

Elly dashed through the crowd until she found Mary, then teased her about Kurt not being able to buy her pie. Mary took a swat at her but missed. The auction started, and as each sale was concluded, Elly and Junior would hoot at the young man who bought the pie and follow him and his lady for a little way and make smooching sounds and laugh and point. Norton Awtrey bought Mary's pie, and Elly and Junior trailed after them until Norton pulled Mary up before him on his horse and rode off.

They ran over to the tent where the cooking contests were held. The jelly and preserves judgings were being concluded, and they hoped to get a taste, but didn't. They crawled under the tables and giggled at the conversations around them. One woman with fat, quivering legs told a funny story to the lady standing next to her about eating pickled beets. She'd eaten a whole jar of pickled beets one night, and when she'd gotten up next morning, "I followed nature's call, you know, and"—her voice lowered—"my urine was all red as blood. I thought, 'My dear Lord, my insides are all eaten up!' I didn't imagine it was those beets. I thought I was going to die!"

Elly and Junior dashed outside and laughed and held each other and laughed.

"Her pee was as red as blood!" squawked Junior.

They staggered around cross-eyed and gulped down gallon after gallon of moonshine and beet juice.

"Thought she was gonna die!" hooted Elly.

6.

As he lowered her toward him, Mary felt the stiff newness of his wool army jacket, brown like the rich brown of his hair, and she swam so stunned in the ocean blue of his eyes that she almost forgot the pie box cradled carefully in her hands. Then she was on the ground and Norton led his stallion off and tethered it to the well. They sat on the rough bench in front of the little school—as empty and quiet and useless as a church on Tuesday. She opened the box and sat the pie on the bench between them and cut a large wedge. When she tried to lift it out, though, the chocolate oozed out the sides and fell back into the pie tin in fat plops. At the point of the wedge, the egg-white topping sank down to the crust. She tried to fork the chocolate filling onto the plate, but it was so runny that it seeped through the tines.

She felt her face go hot and red.

Norton took the plate from her and scooped a couple of bites into his mouth. He gave up on that and took the piece of pie into his hands and took a bite, but a blob of chocolate slopped down onto his pants, so he tossed the pie onto the ground and stood up.

"They can feed that to the dogs."

Mary ran into the school and sat down on a bench in the corner. Tears were in her eyes, and her lungs shuddered and seemed to fill with hot tears, but she didn't cry. Norton came in after her and walked up the center aisle and back, then paced back and forth in front of the windows on the west. When he passed in front of a window, the sun flung his shadow across the room and caught in spangles of fire on his brass buttons.

"Don't take it that way, Mary. What's a pie mean anyhow?" he began. "I mean, there's bigger things than pie sales and Summer Fairs going on in the world now. There's bigger things than Sunday's Hollow happening, and it's crazy to let little things bother you."

"I guess you won't be going to that school in St. Louis now that you've joined the army, will you?" Her voice trembled, but she tried to control her tears, tried not to let the pettiness of the day, of her whole life, intrude now.

He spoke with raw contempt for the university in St. Louis, for all the small things that led to small lives. He didn't mention the war or the Kaiser outright, but he spoke of the great things that a man must face sometime in his life. He didn't say that he might go to the war and die, might never come back, but she felt it strong in his tone as he paced and talked on and on and seemed to grow drunk with the majesty and splendor of young mortality. As he sat next to her on the bench and pulled her up close, she breathed deeply the inebriate air of his glory.

He begged her to make him forget the meanness of the Hollow, to give him one memory to return to.

"Do you love me, Norton?" she asked.

"You bet I do," he said.

He kissed her long and hard on the mouth, bending her neck back until it ached and pressing her lips against her teeth until she was afraid they'd bleed. He pushed her onto her back on the bench and lifted the hem of her dress. She wanted to tell him to stop, but words seemed so useless. It had been such a petty day. When he was on top of her, the weight pressed her shoulder blades against he wooden bench until she thought that she would have to cry out from the pain. She put her hands down to the floor on either side of the bench to keep from rolling off, and that seemed to ease the pain on her shoulders somewhat, too.

When he was finished, he stood up and buttoned his trousers. Mary lay there a minute, then got up and took a couple of tentative steps. She felt something running down her leg, so she turned her back to him and lifted her dress. It was blood. It had already ruined a stocking, and a bright splash of it was soaking into her petticoat. She didn't know what she'd tell her mother. She wept. Norton tossed his handkerchief down on the bench next to her and walked out of the school. She didn't know if he meant it for the tears or the blood, but she used it on the blood.

When she finished and went outside, Norton was waiting on his horse. He stared nervously away into the trees.

She was pretty sure that he didn't love her.

7.

"Better save that to prime the pump, girl. Be a good start on next year," her daddy said.

"But I don't want to spend it *next* year. I want spend it *this* year," Elly whined.

Elly sat in the back of the wagon between George and Viola and clutched the hot, sweaty nickel tight in her palm. The Summer Fair was slipping away from her into the afternoon shadows, and she *had* to spend that last nickel.

"What are you going to buy with it?" asked her momma wearily.

"A bottle of sody pop," Elly lied. Sody pop went too fast. Once you drank it, it was all gone. She wanted something to remember, something that would catch and hold the life of the whole day.

"Mary'll be back any time now," her momma said doubtfully.

"But she ain't back yet! If I see her coming, I'll run back real fast. I promise I'll be back as soon as she is."

Her mother shrugged, "It's your money, I guess."

Elly jumped out of the wagon and ran over toward the tents. She began to feel desperate because many people were leaving, and a few of the tents and booths were starting to come down. She wouldn't buy sody pop. That went too fast. A caramel apple? She could get an apple for herself most any time, so that was five cents just for the caramel. A ride on the merry-go-round? She'd done that three times already.

She was dashing from booth to booth when she noticed a knot of people crowding around a little tent off to the side. Others were walking hurriedly over in that direction. She ran over and dodged around the edge of the crowd trying to see. She tugged at a tall man's sleeve and asked what was going on. He frowned down at her but then craned back toward the tent without answering. She pushed past him and started boring her way through the thicket of legs and hips—butting and elbowing, being snatched back occasionally, but threading her way at last to the inner circle that ringed at a respectful four or five paces a figure slumped in a chair.

It was Billy Lewis: legs thrust out askew, big booted feet pointed curiously inward; one arm dangling at his side, the other curled up delicately on his chest; eyes like a catfish once it's stopped flopping; tongue hanging black and absurdly long straight down to the tip of his chin. At his feet on its side lay a jug still dripping a caustically sweet-smelling liquid.

"Bad corn," someone behind Elly whispered.

Dead.

8.

She watched the slick flanks of the mule jar up and down, left and right with each step as it leaned against the weight and struggled up the road. The six of them in the wagon made a tough pull for one animal. Too, it was a hot August afternoon—like they all were, it seemed—even though there was a bit of a breeze. She opened her legs slightly and pulled subtly at her dress, the hem climbing up her right leg almost to her knee, and the breeze nestled cool between her calves, then thighs. She glanced to the side. John hadn't noticed, and neither had the children. She didn't care anyway. It was she who had gotten up early and prepared the food, hustled the whole menagerie together and got them there in one piece. A body could ask for a bit of comfort, if nothing else, at the end of a day's work.

She looked back into the wagon. George gazed off into the trees, and Viola, the quiet one, was rocked roughly in her sleep by the unsteady lurching of the mule. Mary sat hunched in the corner, bent over like she had a bellyache. Her eyes were wet and red. The Schneider boy hadn't bought her pie. The Awtrey boy was good looking and quite a catch, but you never could tell where a young girl's fancy would take her. There would be other boys. Best let them suffer it out for themselves.

Elly worried her more—huddled in the back as still as a chick peering into a blacksnake's eyes. She had seen the Lewis boy. It was a shame—that young—but then maybe it would teach the other young men of the Hollow a lesson about the dangers of spirits. Elly was young and strong as a colt, but young ones can be scarred so easily. Still, a body must face it sometime. The Lord giveth . . .

She clucked her tongue.

So, another Summer Fair was over. You could almost measure out your life by them. But you could do that with Christmasses or birthdays or New Years or the wearing out of dresses or the way you're a little less strong in the morning and a little more tired each night, so no one thing was that important.

She sighed. Elly would be in the second grade come fall. There wouldn't be any more children, she was sure of that. John had slowed up in a lot of ways. She glanced over at him. He was nodding off, his head dropping slowly and coming back up in jerks. His palsied hand shook slightly on the reins. Everybody said the same thing to her: Seems like John is slowing up an awful lot lately. Well, that would come too, before long, and then she'd have it all alone. No use thinking about it, though. What you could help you worked at, and what you couldn't you suffered through. If there was too much suffering, you died, and then the suffering stopped.

The mule strained up over the crest of a hill, and the wagon began to pick up speed, bouncing and jarring over the ruts and stones. She reached down and pulled out the old horse blanklet at her feet, then slid it under her to make the ride a little easier the rest of the way home.

HORIZON

IT HAD BEEN A LATE FALL—the soft maples had not finished turning by the coming of November—and as Lelia walked up the path away from her house she could feel the sweat rising on her upper lip.

When she got to the road, Kurt Schneider was coming up the hill in his Model-T, which was coughing and backfiring and sliding in and out of the wagon ruts. She waved for him to stop, but he was so intent on making the top of the hill that he hardly took notice of her, just nodded and clutched the wheel with both hands, rearing up off the seat as if he were trying to pull the fuming, sputtering thing up by brute strength. It wasn't until the Model-T finally dropped over the crest of the hill that Lelia let her hand fall slowly to her side.

It was all right, though, she decided. Sour and laconic, Kurt Schneider would have been no comfort. No, he wouldn't have been the one to tell.

Besides, as she turned back and looked down the road that twisted its way through Sunday's Hollow, she could see others coming, first Harvey and Elsa Pimm in their wagon and then the Crossleys, walking, and then another couple and child on foot, too far away to identify but probably the Ridgeways.

The mule pulling the Pimms' wagon didn't make as much noise as Kurt Schneider's Model-T, but with its hooves striking off rocks, its wheezing and panting and snorting as it leaned against the weight of the wagon, it didn't miss by much.

Lelia waved for them to stop. Elsa, thinking she was just being friendly, waved back.

"You going to the celebration, Lelia?" she called above the protests of the mule. Harvey didn't even look over. He wasn't about to let that mule so much as think about stopping until it made the hill.

"It's John!" Lelia hollered as the wagon rumbled on by.

Elsa held tight to the wagon seat with her right hand, pressed her bonnet to her head with her left as she twisted around to shout back at Lelia, "Yes, I know, you poor thing! No better?"

Lelia shook her head slowly.

"No, no better," she said, more to herself than to Elsa, who had turned away anyway, her body held tensely erect on the wagon seat, as if in anticipation of the crest of the hill, or what lay beyond.

In another minute the Crossleys, Albert and Pauline, were drawing near.

"Ain't you going to the big deal in Jerico, Lelia?" Pauline asked, pretending to scratch the side of her nose in order to conceal her harelip.

"It's John," Lelia said, waving vaguely off in the direction of her house.

"Yes, I know, poor thing," she said, echoing Elsa Pimm. "We all have our crosses, sweetheart, but yours is heavier than most. Why don't you get that lazy Opal to spell you a couple of hours so you can come with us and join the fun?"

Even as she was talking, though, Pauline was edging away beside Albert, who obviously was in a hurry to be off.

"No, you all go on," Lelia said.

"You get that lazy Opal to spell you," Pauline repeated, rubbing her nose. Lelia watched them walk on off up the road.

No, George and Opal, her son and daughter-in-law, were already at the picnic, with Elly and Viola, Lelia's two youngest daughters. George needed a break bad as anybody— since John's stroke he had all the heavy work around the farm to do by himself—and she didn't begrudge Opal a little enjoyment. She wasn't as lazy as Pauline said, just moody and highstrung. Elly and Viola? Elly was too young and flighty to be much help with John, and Viola . . . well, the truth was since she caught herself afire cooking bisquits she hadn't been worth much.

Viola'd have more scars than any veteran at the picnic, Lelia'd bet. Norton Autrey had been the only one from the hollow to die, and that was from dysentery. She'd heard Shug Powell talk about walking into that Belleau Wood, the German bullets sounding like bees as they buzzed by him, but he'd been spared. Kenny

Summers, who talked more about the war than anybody, had spent it all in Brooklyn, New York!

1923. How on earth had it gotten to be 1923? It seemed like just yesterday that the war ended: the boys riding up and down the hollow on their horses, whooping and hollering, the sound of gunshots all day and into the night. She'd felt like an old woman then, even though she'd been only thirty-seven. And that was before Viola's accident, before Mary and the Carter boy got married and moved out of the house, before George married Opal and brought her home with him—not a good trade, Mary for Opal. Before John had his stroke. If she'd been an old woman in 1918, what was she now? She was whatever you called a woman who worked herself to death for twenty-three years on a dirt farm in a backwoods Missouri hollow. What was the name for that?

The couple and child—a boy, she could see now, and yes, they were the Ridgeways—were coming closer. She would tell them about John. She'd always felt closer to Kate Ridgeway than to most other women in the hollow, felt a certain kinship since both were outsiders, Kate brought in from Ohio by her husband just as John had brought Lelia against her will from Pennsylvania. Against her will.

Then Lelia noticed that Elmer Ridgeway was wearing his army uniform. He was a veteran, too, she now recalled, although he never talked about it like Kenny Summers or Shug Powell, never wore his uniform even when he first came back from the war. He'd been a lot older than most of the other young men who joined up, and some said he'd returned a bitter man. Yet here he was today in his uniform, heading for the fifth anniversary celebration of Armistice Day. Let him go on.

Let them all go on, Lelia decided, turning away from the road and heading back to the house before the Ridgeways got close enough to make speech necessary. It was a hard life for all of them. They all deserved what little pleasure they could find. No, she wouldn't burden them with her troubles. Besides, Reverend Greene had promised to drop by that afternoon. She could stay with John until then. She'd had him all these years after all. What difference would a couple more hours make?

Lelia walked back up the path and was about to enter the house when she noticed that their dog Sassy's water pan was empty. It was an old enamel five-quart pan they'd brought from Pennsylvania, used so much it'd worn a hole in the bottom edge. But if you put your finger over the hole when you filled it, then tilted it up against something so the hole was above the water line, it'd still hold water enough for Sassy for a day or two. Lelia dipped the pan into the rain barrel at the corner of the house, then set it at an angle up against the barrel. Sassy had learned to drink delicately, not push her nose against the pan, knocking it over.

That's what you had to do in life, Lelia thought. You learned to do what must be done to survive. Didn't mean you liked it—mostly you didn't like it, but still, if you wanted to survive . . .

There'd come that day, though, when, despite all your care, you'd find that something—a big wind maybe—had knocked the pan over, or you'd find the pan sitting there with no water. Someday, despite everything, you'd be caught by surprise.

Lelia went into the house. John was lying there

where she'd left him, on the floor beside the bed. She pulled a chair over next to him and sat down to wait for the Reverend.

She'd been out gathering eggs when it happened, heard it all the way out in the hen house. It'd sounded so loud, like a wall collapsing or a clap of thunder, and when she ran back into the house she couldn't believe it when she found John on the floor. She stood there the longest time, not even breathing, staring, before she suddenly shouted, "John!" But he didn't move.

How had it happened? What had he been trying to do? In the two weeks since he'd had his stroke he hadn't moved a muscle, except for his eyes which rolled blindly left to right, right to left, and his tongue, which mostly pushed back out the broth and mush she tried to feed him. Then after all that time lying there he'd all of a sudden . . . done what? Rolled over and fell out of bed? Maybe he heard her outside working and tried to get up to help.

At first she tried to get him back into bed, but even though he'd wasted away to almost nothing she couldn't manage it by herself. So she let him lie where he fell, put a pillow under his head and sat beside him stroking his face, his waxy flesh growing cooler and cooler under her fingertips. She couldn't believe he was really dead.

That's what puzzled her most as she sat in the chair and stared at him, lying on his side, his head resting on the pillow: not his dying but that she'd been caught off guard by it. She'd been waiting for his death, after all, not just for the fourteen days since his stroke but since before the war. He'd been failing for at least that long— if

she'd *felt* old five years ago, he *was* old by then; she'd
been waiting that long to hear the sound of his falling,
but she had not expected it to sound like thunder, nor to
be so shaken by it, to sit on the floor stroking his face,
saying, *Is he really dead?*

Until that morning if anybody had asked her at
any point over the last twenty-three years of her life what
she thought she'd feel at her husband's death, she would
have told them *relief*, *release*, and something else she
couldn't think of a word for, but until it came to her
revenge would do. But revenge for what?

Oh, she could tell them that, that was easy. She'd
tell them about the little store on the hill in Pennsylvania
where the women would come mornings to buy cloth
and canned goods and dried beans, where their husbands
black with coal dust would stop by after the day shift and
drink coffee and eat cheese and crackers and listen to
John tell his endless stories about his father and the
Indians. She'd tell about the four-room clapboard house
behind the store with the porch running across the front,
hers, until one day John said they were moving to Kansas,
and then the surprise of her life: not John saying he want-
ed to go but her not killing him right there or at least
telling him to go on ahead to Kansas if he wanted to, and
to hell on his way, just leave her be. But no, she up and
went with him, not even making it to Kansas but stop-
ping off in this hollow where men worked themselves to
death with less to show for it than the coal miners in
Pennsylvania, where every day for twenty-three years she
felt like sitting down and crying or by God just dying,
which is what a lot of women did. She'd seen them, men
too—worked until they couldn't anymore, then sat down

and died.

She gazed down at John, his grey face yellow-tinted from the sun beaming through the window curtains she'd made from burlap bags. Burlap bags! She'd been poor in Pennsylvania, too, but never in her life did she hang burlap bags over her windows and call them curtains.

She tried to stare at John with hatred, but couldn't. Why couldn't she? She'd thought she hated the man for twenty-three years for dragging her to Missouri, getting four children on her, each one like a fence post driven deep in the ground, staking her to the hollow like you'd stake out a field that began all green and fertile but got farmed out, old and rocky and worthless, but you were too poor to give it away or turn your back on it because it was all you had, all you were, what your life had come down to after all these years.

Lelia pushed herself up from the chair and went into the kitchen, opened up the pie safe John had bought for her in Clinton and took out the pan black from countless bakings. In it were two large squares of cornbread from last night's supper. She took one and broke it up into a glass, smelled the milk left over from breakfast to see if it was still sweet, poured the milk on top of the cornbread.

She took the glass back into the bedroom, sat down, and began to eat the milk and cornbread with a spoon. But after only one or two bites she stopped, looked at John.

"John!" she said sharply. "You must eat. Get your strength back."

She started to rise up out of her chair with the

glass, but stopped herself.

"I'll swan, woman, are you going to try to feed a dead man?" she asked herself.

What was the matter with her—was she going crazy? She felt light-headed, dizzy, as if that clap of thunder an hour ago had knocked everything out of kilter.

She stared at John—the scar on his forehead where that bad-tempered mare of theirs had run him into a hickory limb, years and years ago, the hair once black as coal dust but now thin and wispy like white corn silk, his flesh, a mottled grey since his stroke but now in death with an almost pearly lustre to it. She felt like lying down beside him and touching his face.

She felt like crying. Crying! She hadn't cried for twenty-three years, not since that first day they'd ridden into the hollow and she stepped into the drafty little cabin John had traded the wagon for, and she'd realized as she stared around her that she was looking at the rest of her life. She thought she had her bitterness, her hatred to keep her from crying after that, but where had the hatred gone to? Now, when she should have felt *release*, *revenge*, she only felt like crying.

She gazed down at her husband, stifling an urge to lie beside him and hold his hand; instead, she bent down from the chair and touched one fingertip to the cool dry flesh of his upturned palm.

*

As she walked up the path toward the road, she tried to guess the time by the length and angle of the shadows. But she had never been very good at it. John had wanted to buy her a wall clock, but she refused; she didn't want any reminders of how much time, how much of her life, she was losing to him and Sunday's Hollow. John, though, he would cock his eye at the shadow thrown by a fence post, rub his chin, then announce the time. Then he'd pull out the big nickle-plated pocket watch he always called his "railroad watch," although Lelia didn't know what John had ever had to do with the railroad, and check his estimate against it. He was never more than a couple of minutes off. One day, though, Lelia peeked around the burlap curtains and saw him quickly check his watch before walking over to George and "gauging" the time by a pitchfork handle. She didn't know whether to laugh or cry. She once told Kate Ridgeway that she had given birth to four children but she had five on her hands—and sometimes she thought John was the biggest baby of them all.

When she got to the road, she saw that it must be later than she thought because people were streaming back down the hill from the direction of Jerico. She could make out the Ridgeways and the Stadlers, and there were others behind them. They all had their chores to do while there was still daylight.

Suddenly, Lelia was startled to realize that, much closer than the Ridgeways or Stadlers, a solitary figure in a black suit and black broad-brimmed hat was moving in and out of the shadows lying across the road, was almost upon her. Reverend Greene. What a stroke of luck that he'd be right there the moment she stepped into the road to look for him. Or was it luck? Lelia thought that maybe there was no luck or coincidence but that everything in the world existed to baffle her.

"Hello, Lelia."

"Reverend Greene," she nodded, running the back of her hand across her forehead. How on earth could the man bear that wool suit? It could well be a late summer day instead of November. She even imagined she could hear bees buzzing in the distance.

"And how is John today?"

"John passed on this morning, Reverend," Lelia said.

"Oh!" He whipped the hat off his head and pressed it against his chest. "I'm so sorry, Lelia. I know this is a terrible thing to be—"

He suddenly stopped what he was saying and frowned, turned his head to the side as if listening for something.

Then Lelia heard it, too. It *was* a bee, or a hornet perhaps, some distant but incessant buzzing, faint but growing.

The Reverend remembered himself and turned back to her.

"I know it's a terrible thing to be bereft of your husband, Lelia," he said, "but the good Lord in His mercy knows when it's time to end the suffering. John is at peace now."

He no sooner finished his last words than he whirled and looked back up the road, at the Ridgeways perhaps, who were almost upon them. But no, he was obviously listening to the strange buzzing, still at a distance but too loud for a bee or hornet or a whole nest of hornets.

He didn't even acknowledge the Ridgeways when

they walked up and stopped beside him and Lelia.

"Lelia?" Kate asked tentatively.

"Yes," Lelia nodded. "John's gone. He went this morning."

"Oh you poor—" Kate began, then stopped.

She turned to look back up the hill, in the direction of the sound, too loud to call it a buzzing now, filling the whole sky.

And then Lelia saw it, coming at them over the treetops, an enormous bird, gliding more swiftly than a storm cloud and roaring like spring thunder. Reverend Greene gripped his hat with both hands and flinched as if expecting a mighty blow. Lelia wanted to throw herself on the ground but was too frightened to move. All of them in unison ducked their heads as the thing passed over them. The Ridgeway boy let out a shout, and shouts went up from the people up and down the road—not shouts of fear, no, of awe and joy.

"Aeroplane," Elmer Ridgeway said, trying to sound matter-of-fact but his voice trembling. "Saw a lot of them in the war."

Lelia had never seen an aeroplane before. Probably you could count on the fingers of one hand those of her friends and neighbors who had.

"The first aeroplane in Sunday's Hollow!" Kate Ridgeway exclaimed.

"This is a new world," the Reverend said solemnly.

*

Together Lelia and Reverend Greene, a little man

over sixty who looked like a wizened boy in his black suit, managed to get John back up on the bed. Then they knelt by the bed and folded their hands, and Reverend Greene began to pray, speaking of God's plan, changes, a time to live and a time to die.

It was then, not because of the Reverend's words but because John had begun to smell, that Lelia began to live in time again, which surprised her because until time moved forward once more she had not been aware that it had stopped earlier that morning in a clap of thunder—or if not stopped gotten all mixed up so that she couldn't tell if she was living now or five years ago or twenty-three years ago.

But the smell told her. She was living now, in time, while John was then, out of time. Even though she was close enough to reach out and touch his cheek it was as if she were moving away from him at such speed that it hurt to breathe, oh yes, it hurt so, the pain suddenly was so awful that she gasped "Oh God!" so loud that the Reverend stopped his praying and looked at her with concern and said, "Lelia?"

It was a question, but she didn't know what the answer was until until she said it: "I loved him."

At the instant of that terrible confession, Lelia felt her life break in half, or rather sensed with something like prescience and certainly horror that despite feeling like an old woman she'd lived only half her life, the first half in self-deception and bafflement and the second half, the half to come, in understanding. Understanding, she knew, was to be her punishment, for chief among all that was now so clear to her was the realization that she could recover from death but she could never recover from love.

"A new world," the Reverend murmured as if he had been reading her thoughts, and Lelia nodded and started to say yes, but then she saw that he wasn't talking to her but to himself as he looked past her toward the window. She turned and looked, and even though she couldn't see it through the burlap curtain, she could hear it coming back, the aeroplane, growing louder and louder. In her new world of understanding she understood even this, and for an instant she was up there with the man in the aeroplane, with awe and despair racing toward a horizon that never drew nearer, that she would never reach.

THE MAN WHO
CAME TO LOVE THE HEAT

BY LATE JULY OF '33, the temperature had reached a high of 117 degrees. The land had been thirty days without rain, and, shrinking in horror from itself, was scarred with a chaos of cracks wide enough to lose a leg in. The soil had faded from rich April black to May brown, then grey in June and an ascetic bone white in July.

The corn crop was not ruined—there was no crop to ruin. There were no beans in July of '33, no potatoes, and few onions. The farmers joked that their wheat was baked before its flour had reached the ovens.

Harvey Pimm walked between what should have been rows of his corn crop, each step scuffing up an ashy cloud of dust which expanded, hovered, and dropped back in exhaustion to the earth. He hated the day of his birth and the day of his father's birth. The sun blasted down, and Harvey felt its ruthless heat heavy on his head and shoulders, his feet cooking in the earth-kiln.

And then it happened.

A sudden change swept over Harvey, as when a March wind turns from north to south and brings the spring. But the change was not in the wind—there was no wind—nor in the sun or sky. The change was in Harvey, as if something snapped, released in him. The vise of hatred that clinched his heart fell away in perfect halves, bitter bile evaporated in the sun, and Harvey felt the heat enter, become a part of him, flow with his blood and cleanse, wash over his bones, innards, and muscles.

Harvey was in an ecstacy of heat. He breathed heat deeply in his lungs, felt it on his lips, smelled it in the sweat of his moustache. It ran in glories of sweat down his neck and shoulders and sides. The muscles of his legs were massaged to a warm jelly by the heat and slowly gave way, and he fell to his knees in the heat-kissed earth. He raised his arms high in praise of the sun, opened his hands to let the heat paint every crease of his palms and fingers.

He was in that posture when he heard his wife, Elsa, stamping up between the dusty furrows.

"What in the Lord's good name, Harvey? . . . Good Gawwd! He's done took heatstroke!"

She came around behind him and grabbed him under the arms and tried to pull him to his feet, but he let his weight go limp, and she couldn't budge him.

Elsa ran around in little circles like a frightened chicken, her hands pulling at the hair behind her temples.

"Lord God, Harvey, don't die on me now. I'm too old and beat to find another husband!"

Then she stopped running and seemed to collect herself. She leaned down over Harvey and placed a hand on his shoulder.

"Don't you worry, Harv, I'm going to send George Workman to get the Doc for you. Just as soon as those two pans of cornbread come out of the stove."

She went on back to the house, and Harvey let himself float up to the sun on waves of heat, steep there in its riches.

Some time later—Harvey seemed to be losing all sense of time—Elsa was back with Opal Workman, George's wife.

Opal Workman bent over him, fanning him with her apron.

"Lord love you, hon," she crooned.

Then Opal and Elsa were down on their knees, the three of them forming a triangle with the women facing Harvey. Harvey had been expecting a good deal of praying ever since Opal showed up. Praying was about Opal's favorite thing—it was one of the reasons Harvey steered clear of her whenever possible. But today he could accept that, too, along with everything else. In fact, when Opal and Elsa began praying, he found it all very interesting— they seemed to be groping toward the same spirit he'd found in the sun—and he was proud of Elsa, who was holding her own pretty good although she'd had a lot less practice at it than Opal.

When they'd finished praying, Opal suggested they had better try to get Harvey into the house. It might be who knows how long before George got back with the Doc, and by that time . . .

Opal got on the right side of Harvey and Elsa on the left. They took him by the arms and heaved. Harvey let his muscles go completely lax, let his body weight hang dead as before, but the two women, groaning and struggling, managed to get him up. When he felt himself being stood on his feet, Harvey threw out his right arm and then his left. Opal hit the ground heading toward the southwest and Elsa the southeast. Harvey sat gently back down in the rocky furrow, tilted his face up to the smiling sun.

Elsa scrambled to her feet, came up close to him, and peered into his eyes.

"Why, I don't think you had a heat-stroke, Harvey Pimm. I don't think you had a stroke at all."

With that she reached over and grabbed Harvey by the right earlobe, gave it a tug. Harvey smiled up at the sky. Elsa gave the earlobe a good pull, at the same time pinching down with thumb and forefinger. Harvey was so at ease, lulled by his rhapsody of heat, that he felt they could work him like taffy. Then Elsa really put her weight into it, rotating and throwing her hip into Harvey, pulling the ear over her right shoulder like she was hefting a sack of oats onto her back by its neck.

Harvey came up fast, eyes watering, and was set to clip Elsa in the back of the head with his elbow when Opal broke in.

"Merciful heaven, Elsa! You'll tear the poor man's head clean off. If he ain't had a heat stroke, he's at least gone crazy. Either way he's one of the Lord's afflicted. We must be merciful, Elsa. Jesus would want it so."

Elsa let go of the ear and Harvey sat back down, having already forgiven her. The sun forgave everything.

"Well," said Elsa grudgingly, "I'll wait until the Doc gets here. But he better've had a stroke, that's all. If all he is is crazy, there'll be hell to pay."

By the time George Workman got back from

Warsaw with Dr. Baldwin, Elsa and Opal were back in the house. The four of them started back across the field toward Harvey. The Doc looked into his eyes, felt the back of his neck, his forehead, opened his mouth and looked in, took his pulse, felt the muscle of his arm and leg. Put his ear to Harvey's chest and listened to his heart. "Doesn't look like any stroke to me."

"Hunh!" Elsa snorted and headed for Harvey, but Opal cut her off.

"Hear him out, Elsa. Don't do nothing rash. What do you figure it is, Doc? Do you figure he's gone crazy?"

Doctor Baldwin shook his head, closed his right eye, and cocked his left wide open, canted toward Harvey. With his bushy grey eyebrows he looked like a sagacious old owl.

"Crazy? No, we don't use that word anymore. The fact is, I just got back from a medical convention in St. Louis. The AMA."

He paused for this to sink in on the Workmans and Pimms, but they didn't react. Probably never heard of the AMA. Never even heard of it! What he got for devoting his life to a bunch of hicks. He'd grown up in Jefferson City and could have opened his practice there, lived in real society, but no, he went where he was needed most. Schweitzer didn't have a damn thing on him.

"The AMA," he started to explain, but the sun was so hot! "—well forget it. The thing is, I went to this session on Sigmund Freud, Jew fellow from Germany. Don't expect you've heard of him?—no, course not. Well, this Jew fellow has come up with a lot of interesting explanations behind why people get sick in the head. We don't say 'crazy' anymore, we say 'sick in the head.'"

"I've heard of that," George Workman said.

"Sure. Anyway, it's all too complicated to go into, but it's quite clear to me that what's happened is that Harvey here's got himself pole-axed by an Oedipus complex."

"He et what?"

"Who pole-axed him?"

"Never mind. It's one of these things you don't have a ghost of a chance of understanding without special training. Besides, I wouldn't dare go into it in mixed company, if you get my drift. The important thing is, there's no need to get all excited or chain him up or anything unless he gets violent, which is highly unlikely to happen with this particular kind of sick in the head. By the way, Harvey's parents are gone, aren't they?"

"They went several years ago. Both of 'em," Elsa said.

"Good! The only folks in real danger around someone bit by the Oedipus bug is the victim's father and mother. Now for God's sake don't ask me to explain that. You wouldn't believe me if I told you."

George pulled at his right earlobe.

"Well, what do you reckon we oughtta do, then, Doc?" he asked.

"It's pretty simple, actually. You talk to him, get him to talk to you. About his childhood, preferably. Get him to fess up to some purely rotten thing he did as a kid, then, bingo!, this Oedipus thing'll clear right up. I'd do it for you, but I've got patients back in town waiting on me. Besides, too damn hot out here for me."

They walked back to the house, and Elsa gave Doctor Baldwin one of the pans of cornbread and a fifty cent piece they'd been holding back for an emergency.

Elsa went back out to the field feeling pretty good. It could have been something serious to where she'd have to tend the farm by herself or go on the hunt for a new husband, at her age. But it turns out that a little talk, and Harvey would be right back on his feet.

Elsa sat down on the ground next to Harvey, took his hand and petted it, then dropped it in embarrassment. She cleared her throat.

"Well, Harvey, you want to tell me what it was you done when you were a little kid?"

She wouldn't put anything past him, then or now.

But Harvey didn't say anything. He angled his head slightly forward and to the right so that the sun could run down his shirt collar, caressing halfway down his chest.

"Anything you'd like to get off your chest, Harv? Was it some mean thing you done as a boy? Anything at all you'd like to talk about? I'm here to listen. Got anything to say, Harvey? . . . Harvey? . . . Harvey? . . . Shit fire!"

Elsa got up and walked off in disgust, came back with a bucket of water and dumped it over Harvey's head. It felt like acid scalding over him. He lashed out and knocked the bucket flying. Elsa got down on her knees and hissed.

"Sit there and die then, you son-of-a-bitch! Die!"

*

Harvey breathed deeply in relief, alone with his sun again. It lay a fat ball of red fire on the shoulder of the earth, painting the field in amber and rose. But despite its brilliance, Harvey could already feel its power waning. He stretched out his arms to take in all of its warmth, but it began to fade, darken, drown in a sea of gold and violet.

When it was fully gone, Harvey stood trembling in the wasted field. He was dizzy and confused and fell twice on the way back to the house. When he walked through the door, Elsa rushed up to him—not sure whether to hug him in relief or slap him crosseyed for scaring her so—but he shoved by her and lifted the water bucket to his lips. He drank in great gulps, with the water splashing over his face and shoulders and darkening the floor. When he finished drinking, he grabbed up a hunk of dry cornbread and swallowed it in four bites, hardly chewing. This set him to coughing and gagging, and finally he dropped to his knees on the floor, vomited loudly and dismally, then fell in a heap and lay in a tormented sleep the rest of the night.

*

Elsa hoped that with sleep the fit would pass, but when the dawn sun stepped through the door and tapped him shyly on the shoulder, he greeted it like a returned lover, with serene and absolute passion. He wandered dreamily into the barren field, fell to his knees once more and worshipped the east sky, sweat already beginning to slick his face and shoulders.

Soon, word began to spread throughout Sunday's Hollow that Harvey Pimm had gone queer as a three-dollar bill. Such an occurrence was not altogether unheard of in the Hollow and, in normal times, might not have attracted a good deal of attention, but with the drought the farmers had very little to do except curse God. So as the day, wore on more and more began to drift over in the direction of the Pimm's farm.

Almost without exception, the women would give the excuse that they were coming over to help Elsa with this new burden, while the men claimed they'd come to "diagnose" Harvey's problem. ("How do you diagnose this here thing, Bob?" "Well sir, I diagnose it this way . . ." "That so? Well, what do you think of that diagnosis, Albert?" "I don't think it's worth a hill of beans. Now here's the way I diagnose it . . .")

Heatstroke and crazy were the two most obvious diagnoses, but there were others. Shug Powell said that Harvey was probably just drunk. Shug was pretty much obligated to say that because his wife, Dolly, was a hard-shell Baptist who ascribed to alcohol all the evils of the world, and Shug would've caught hell for it if he'd let pass an opportunity to point out the manifest depredations of spirits.

Spirits was the answer, all right, declared Albert Crossly, but Shug had the wrong variety in mind. Harvey was possessed of the devil, Albert swore. A whole gang of Gypsies had passed through Benton County not a week before, he'd heard. They'd been met at the Cole Camp city limits by townsmen armed with shotguns and rifles and ready to use them—delighted to use them—and the Gypsies had turned tail, probably zapping Harvey with the evil eye before they left. But Harvey hadn't been to Cole Camp in months, Kurt Schneider, Harvey's broth-er-in-law, objected. No problem, according to Albert. The evil eye is good up to seven miles, seven being a magic number for devil-worshipping Gypsies. But Albert, they pointed out, Cole Camp was a good deal more than seven miles from the Hollow. No problem. The evil eye travels especially good in hot, dry air. Twenty, twenty-five miles would be no problem at all.

If Harvey had come up nose to nose with a Gypsy, it might have been a different story, but nobody could much buy the evil eye being flung half-way across Benton County theory.

"No, that ain't even close to it," said Kenny Summers, who had a different idea. "It's marijuana. Nigger jazz singers've been bringing it back from Europe by the suitcase-full. New York's already eaten up with it. The whole East Coast is shot. It's creeping along this way. Just a matter of time. Harvey here's only the first. Dope fiend, that's his problem."

Nobody much knew what to make of that theory, but they had a few thoughts about Kenny Summers, who had been the second volunteer out of the Hollow during World War I, right behind Norton Autrey. Except Norton had had enough pride to at least set his feet down on French soil before dying of dysentery, whereas Kenny had spent the war and two more years afterward at Ft. Hamilton, Brooklyn, shuffling papers. When he finally returned to Sunday's Hollow, he lay claim to anything that had anything to do with New York City, the East Coast, or anything that passed near or over them. This was the same Kenny Summers who couldn't pick his nose if you loaned him a finger.

Anyway, everybody pretty much dismissed the marijuana theory out of hand, just because of the source. Shug Powell was especially interested in moving the conversation on to something else because if his wife heard of it she might take up the anti-dope cause along with the prohibition crusade, and then where would he be? A well-known creek whose named can't be mentioned in polite company, that's where.

All in all, the neighbors had a good time of it, and Harvey didn't much mind, either. He listened to their talk with something like indifferent amusement, but he couldn't understand why they gathered around him as their center when the center of all things—mother and father of us all—stood in perfect fiery splendor in the sky.

It was just when the diagnosing was getting a little old that the men hit on something else to keep them out in that blistering hot field. They began to wager how long Harvey could sit out there without (1) passing clean out or (2) flat dying. At first the wagers were of the simple, two-party variety: "I'll bet you one lonely dime that Harv'll pass out by two o'clock this afternoon." "I'll be happy to take that ten cents from you." "Harvey'll be dead by sundown." "Here's two bits that says he won't." So many wanted to get in on it, though, that it was finally decided that everybody'd put his name and an hour ("between two and three this p.m.") on a slip of paper, and toss it in a hat along with a quarter, winner take all. Actually they had two hats, a dime one and a quarter one, the more expensive pot for dying.

The only problem that remained was that somebody would have to be there all day long to record when Harvey passed out or flat died. They'd just about finished drawing up the schedule of "watchers" when Reverend Greene showed up. This caused considerable consternation because no one had seen him coming until he was right up on them, so nobody had a chance to light off across the field and avoid an inevitable and quite likely considerable spate of preaching. Reverend Greene had taken over the preacher's job at New Hope Baptist from his father, who had retired a few years before. He was a young man, early thirties, strong and tireless. He got heated up fast and stayed hot a long time. He wasn't all to the bad, though. He could be quite entertaining come revival time. Last spring he'd worked up a rage and chased the devil around the church, howling and clawing at the air until he finally lighted on young Junior Schneider, dragged him out of his pew and began walloping him with a Broadman Hymnal until they finally managed to pull him off. And poor Junior, for once, hadn't even been drunk.

The Reverend didn't wait until he was up to Harvey, but launched into his sermon at about thirty feet, and by the time he was amongst them, his theme was pretty clear. Harvey was a lost lamb being called home. A sinner who'd seen the light and been overwhelmed by its glory. Struck blind on the road to Damascus.

"—got his eyes on heaven and his soul with the Lo-o-ord, and his body just ain't caught up to it yet. He don't have no time for us when he's living and loving with Jeeeee-sus."

Reverend Greene had been at it long enough for those on the outer edges of the circle to begin entertaining notions of slinking away when their attention was drawn to the McKutchern twins, Don and Dan, who'd do anything for a dime but had never been known to hold a job for more than two weeks straight, between them. They had dragged some wooden frames across the field, along with a section of old canvas. Reverend Greene managed to ignore them at first, but when they began to hammer the frames together, then stretch the canvas across the top, it quite naturally distracted him just a bit from his preaching. He seemed on the verge of flying off at them when they threw their tools down and walked off. They were back in a few minutes, however, and when they leaned a little cardboard sign up against the front of the rude stand, it was plain what they were up to.

"ICEWATER 5cent a GLASS."

"And for a quarter we might find something else to slip in there," Don McKutchern winked to Junior Schneider.

Reverend Greene was furious.

"Free enterprise, preacher, that's all this is," Dan McKutchern insisted. "That's why this country is in such a mess now—too much FDR and not enough free enterprise."

"Moneychangers! You're profaning the house of God!"

"Hell, Rev, this ain't no house of God. This is just Harvey Pimm's cornfield."

Reverend Greene almost had a stroke himself then. He did a melodramatic buckdance around the stand, kicked it once, then just dove straight into it. Most of the stand and all of Don McKutchern fell on top of him and a glancing one-by-four severed the bottom quarter-inch of his right earlobe, and that was all of the Reverend Greene's preaching—for that day at least.

It took the McKutcherns only a couple of minutes to get the stand back up, and they did a fair nickel business and an even better quarter business for about the next half-hour, until the womenfolk got wind of what was going on and marched out into the field and hauled their men off to home.

The McKutcherns said they'd be back the next day with more to drink and food too—bologna sandwiches and popcorn and candy bars—and Don McKutchern said that he knew where he could lay his hands on a cotton candy machine in Warsaw.

*

The McKutcherns didn't come back the next day, which wasn't at all surprising since they couldn't keep their minds on any one thing, especially involving work, for much longer than it'd take a blind man to bat an eye.

But then there really was no need for them to come back, because no one else went back either. A crazy man can hold a community's interest for only so long. They had done all the diagnosing they were capable of that first day. Even the "watchers," who had come early to see when Harvey keeled, left at eleven because no one had wagered that Harvey would last past the 10:00-11:00 slot. If he could last that long, well, sitting in the sun just might be something Harvey could do better than most folks. He was welcome to it.

But they came back four days later when word got out that Wesley Tucker had contacted some reporter at the *Kansas City Star* about Harvey, who, Wesley told the reporter, was a genuine medical curiosity and was about to break the world sun-sitting record.

So people showed up in their Sunday best after practicing their smiles and rehearsing what they'd say to the *Star* reporter, who never showed up.

"There you have Sunday Hollow's problem in a nutshell," Wesley said. "No respect from the press. Somebody from Sedalia or Jeff City or Springfield scratches his ass and reporters from Kansas City will fall all over themselves writing about it and putting a picture of his behind on page one. But if Jesus Christ decided to pay a visit to Sunday's Hollow and bring his daddy with him, it'd be worth a big yawn to the boys in KC."

Folks pretty much decided that Wesley Tucker had never talked to any Star reporter. They couldn't decide if they were madder at Wesley for pulling another of his crackbrain schemes or themselves for falling for it. They weren't going to fall for another one, that was for sure. They'd leave the field to Harvey.

*

That suited Harvey just fine. He didn't really mind the attention—the people were no more bothersome than the gnats that played about him—and he even half-listened with wry amusement to some of their talk. Only when someone came between him and the sun did Harvey feel irritation flare to rage. But then as soon as the person moved on, and the sun shone down full and bright and loving on him, Harvey would swoon back into his hot and languid grace.

So time passed, with Harvey spending his days in sun-struck splendor and his nights in water-gorged despair.

It took a full week before Elsa finally had had enough. She tromped up the dead furrows and planted herself firmly before him, arms crossed and chin thrust out like a rifle butt.

"It seems to me like, Harvey Pimm," she began, "this being crazy is all right for them that can afford it, but it seems to me like if you love it out here so much that you could at least do a little work while you're being crazy. You know I still have to do the cooking and the washing and the sewing and cleaning up your puke. It seems to me like I shouldn't have to do all that and then spend half my day hauling water and tending the garden to boot. Well, Harvey Pimm, I just want you to know that you may be crazy, but I'm not getting much out of it!"

And then she walked off, kicking up little explosions of dust all the way back to the house.

Two days after Elsa's speech, Kurt Schneider came out into the field. Kurt was Harvey's brother-in-law; he owned the farm just down the road. He and Harvey had never been close because Kurt was sort you just don't get close to. He was a laconic man, with a hint of bitternes and cynicism just behind his close-lipped smile. He had landed in France in the last months of the war just in time to lose three fingers on his right hand, and it was said that he had an ugly scar on his right hip and leg, but Harvey had never seen it.

Kurt stared down at Harvey and rubbed his chin.

Finally he said, "You just quit, didn't you, Harvey? It just broke you."

Harvey turned his face out of Kurt's shadow and caught full the heat of the sun.

"You hear every word I'm saying, don't you Harvey? You hear, but you don't give a damn because you just quit. Ain't that it? That's it all right. I guess it was just too much trouble to use the shotgun or a rope, and there ain't enough water in the creek to drown a puppy in, so this is the way it's going to be—just sit here, just stop. Maybe you've got the right idea after all, I don't know. I don't know why any sane man would want to face another day in this god-awful world, so maybe you hit it there. But don't think you're fooling me. I know you ain't crazy. You just quit."

Kurt paused, but Harvey said nothing, so Kurt looked off toward the west, shrugged.

"Hot. Man oh man, hot. Yep, you're doing real well in the fire, Harvey. Maybe we'll get a chance to see how well you do in the flood. Change is in the air, Harvey. Feel it? Rain coming, I expect."

Then Kurt left.

Harvey shuddered, turned his face toward the west, where a pinkish haze deepened to purple, then slate grey at the horizon. He turned back up to the sun, which caressed him, comforted him. But Harvey was frightened.

That night, the ninth night of his rapture, after gorging himself sick with water and raw turnips, Harvey ran back out into the field, ran in great stumbling arcs of terror. Above him, a huge wedge of black moved slowly from the west across the top of the world and devoured, one by one, the winking stars.

Hours later, instead of a golden shield advancing before the dawn, the sky gradually lightened to reveal brooding clouds like dank, moldy cotton. Harvey felt like a hurled stone. He felt nothing inside but rock-dry bones ready to explode into dust. Dizzy and weak, he fell back onto the earth and could not move.

Then it started. Huge drops plopped onto the ashy field and sent up bursts of dust, leaving little craters in the earth. One hit Harvey in the face and he cried out in pain. He lay dazed and watched the drops grow in number as they darted down at him until they were legion upon legion, a host of arrows falling from the heights of heaven straight down upon him and his land.

When the rain finally stopped, Harvey pulled himself up out of the mud and walked back to the house.

"Damn but I'm hungry," he said to Elsa.

*

The Reverend Greene said that what it was was that Harvey had been baptised by the rains of God. He had sinned and had suffered for his sin in the fires of God's sun and then had been washed clean by the waters of the Lord, and now he could join the world of men again.

George Workman said that he'd always had a theory that after the Garden of Eden God realized that man would never be satisfied with perfection, so He broke everything a little bit. And there for a while Harvey just got caught in the crack of things.

Kurt Schneider had a different opinion, and so did many others. Folks discussed Harvey's spell for a good while after that, but then the talk began to die down. Still, for years to come they watched Harvey pretty close for any signs that the craziness was coming again, but as far as anyone could tell, Harvey was just as normal as all his friends and neighbors.

KOHLRABI

RUBY GLOVER WAS STILL SPRY enough at sixty-eight to chase down a frying hen in her back yard. She'd trip one up with a long wire bent into a hook on one end, then stretch its neck across the tree stump with the wire and bring the ax down with merciful suddenness. A fine spray of blood would dot the ground as the body flopped about the yard. She always felt very sorry for the chicken then, but that didn't stop her from eating it with great relish and sucking its bones.

Ruby Glover had always been a friendly sort even before her husband died, but in the dozen years since Alexander was gone she opened herself to folks with a special warmth—she needed *them* then. She didn't impose, didn't make a nuisance of herself like some old widows have a habit of doing, but her door was always open, and if someone needed an ear to bend, she was there. Most any day you could see some of her old cronies or some of the children of Jerico cross the little foot bridge spanning

the gulley—dry in all but the wettest seasons of the year—
that ran between her house and the blacktop.

Anyway, it wasn't too much of a surprise when
she found the peck basket half filled with lettuce, onions
and radishes on her front porch right beside her rocker. It
wasn't the first basket, either. She had found the first one
over two weeks ago—right about the first of June—and
since then there had been two others. The one that she
found this morning made four altogether. It all added up
to a mystery.

"It's a mystery to me," she would say to Opal
Workman and the other girls in her church Circle. "I just
can't imagine."

"I think Ruby's got her a beau," Opal teased after
the third basket.

Ruby blushed bright as a radish, and that was the
last she mentioned it to her friends.

Ruby touched her hand to her hair before she
remembered that her hands were floury from kneading
dough. She blushed again to think that there might be
just the slightest grain of truth in what Opal said. In fact,
just that morning she'd seen Roland Daniels stalk away
from her house across the footbridge, and when she
looked out on the porch—there was the fourth basket.

Roland Daniels. She barely knew the man. She cer-
tainly had never encouraged him in any way. Once he had
repaired a broken chair for her. He did odd jobs like that
and had a little farm three-quarters of a mile or so east of
Jerico in Sunday's Hollow.

She was all in a dither. She went into the front
room and distractedly began straightening the furniture.
She didn't know what she'd do if she ever caught him in

the act. She couldn't possibly . . .

Ruby caught her breath. Out the front door she saw Roland Daniels pause uncertainly on the blacktop before the footbridge. Ruby moved back into the shadows away from the front door. But then Roland turned away and walked off west.

Ruby was stunned. What could the man possibly be thinking? It wasn't as if she'd never talked to a man since Alexander died, but this man here—Roland Daniels—had bought her four baskets of vegetables. Gifts is what they were—gifts from a widower to a widow woman.

But she had no time to think about that because there was Roland back in front of the footbridge! He paused again, seemed to teeter toward the house, then lurched off east toward Jerico. In the course of the next hour, Roland passed the house a half-dozen more times, pausing each time before the footbridge, then stalking off in one direction or another. Ruby began to feel sorry for the man. Her legs grew tired of standing, so she sat back on the davenport and watched out the window.

At midday, after about the eighth try, Roland gathered himself and charged across the footbridge. Panicked, Ruby fled into the kitchen. She heard him walk up on the porch and hesitate, then he knocked softly—two little pecks at the door. Ruby pretended not to hear. He knocked louder. She thought if she remained very still he might go away. He banged on the door.

"Miss Glover," he called through the door.

She sighed and, all aflutter, walked into the front room. He smiled at her through the screen door and touched a huge browned hand to his hat. It was a new hat—beige with a dark green band—but it went poorly with his old wrinkled dark blue suit, white shirt and crudely knotted black tie.

"Good morning, Miss Glover ma'am," he said with a slight bow and touched the brim of his hat again.

"Mrs. Glover," she corrected, then immediately felt bad because she feared that she sounded rude.

"Mrs. Glover, ma'am."

He grinned sheepishly and stared up at the right hinge of the screen door.

"A widow twelve years this September twenty-two," she sighed. She didn't know why she'd said it.

He took his hat off and seemed to make a vague attempt to cover his heart with it, but missed. It wound up resting in the general vicinity of his liver.

"My wife was gone six years this March..."

His voice trailed off, and he resumed grinning sheepishly. She could tell that he didn't know what to say.

"You've been leaving off the baskets," she offered. "It was neighborly, but you shouldn't have."

"Oh, I had more than I could use. Don't think nothing at all about it. Before too long I'll have sweet corn and tomatoes, and I'll bring you some of those."

"You don't need to do that, Mr. Daniels. I've got a garden of my own."

"How about some squash?"

"Really . . . more than I can use."

"Green peppers?"

"I don't eat them normally. They repeat so."

"Need more onions?"

He began to list off seemingly every edible plant grown in that part of Missouri, but with each item she gave back a polite "no."

"Kohlrabi," he said finally.

Ruby hesitated.

"Kohlrabi?"

"Yes ma'am. Got more than I know what to do with. In fact I never touch the stuff. My wife, she used to eat it, but these six years I just grow it and let the worms have it."

"I haven't tasted kohlrabi in years," she said. "I used to fix it for Mr. Glover."

Roland laughed joyously. "Well, I'll bring you kohlrabi till the cows come home!"

"No, you needn't do that."

"Surely I will. It just goes bad. It's just cabbage to me, and I won't eat cabbage."

"You really don't need to put yourself to any bother."

"No bother."

"But then if you just let it go bad . . ."

"No bother at all," he laughed.

*

That was Saturday. On Monday Roland brought a peck basket brim-full of lettuce, turnips, carrots, and cucumbers. No kohlrabi. He apologized mightily. His memory wasn't as sharp as it used to be, he said. A person that lives alone has no one to hone his wits on, he said. Ruby understood.

On Wednesday he placed in her reluctant arms two jars of honey and, rolled in newspaper, two cleaned carp he'd caught on the creek. He was miserable at forgetting the kohlrabi again. If she was ever by his place, she could pick up more than she'd ever dream of eating, he promised. She didn't reply one way or the other.

On Friday he knocked on her front door, tipped his hat, and said that he'd just been to Clinton in Carl Crossley's pickup, sold four hogs. Could he come in and chat a bit?

"I don't know if it'd be quite proper," she said.

He grinned and nodded and pawed at the porch floor with the muddy, cracked toe of a boot. He told her he'd be sure to bring that mess of kohlrabi first thing next week. In the meantime, if she ever took a notion to stop in at his place, he'd give her a gunny sack full. Ruby said she was hardly ever out that way.

But it was just the next day, Saturday, that Ruby paid a visit to George and Opal Workman in Sunday's Hollow, a mile east of Jerico on the blacktop. They ate deviled eggs and a mess of wilted lettuce for dinner. Then Ida Tucker came over and the three women crocheted and gossiped on the side porch the rest of the afternoon. After Ida left, Opal fried up some chicken and, she, George, and Ruby ate chicken and gravy and bisquits for supper.

Ruby helped clean up the supper dishes then started back up the blacktop for Jerico. The thought of Roland Daniels and his kohlrabi had not crossed her mind until she came opposite the narrow dirt road—hardly more than a path—that branched off north of the blacktop. She knew that it wasn't more than a quarter-mile to his place. On a whim, she turned and started up the road.

It was nearing twilight, and the trees laid their

shadows at her feet as she walked up the narrow road. It was a warm evening, the last day of spring. The breeze whispered secrets to the hickories and maples and elms, and soft things, young things, grew up green from the earth.

It was only a few minutes until the path widened, and she saw Roland's house slouched against the darkening bank of trees. She hesitated. Why had she come? A woman alone to nearly a stranger's house, the day almost gone? It was a foolish thing, but she might as well go on now, having come this far.

Roland's house looked as if it had grown old and forlorn with its owner. Blackish-gray, it had never had a coat of paint apparently, and wooden shingles curved up like dry leaves on the roof. The porch was littered with rags, bushel baskets in a stack, a worn sofa of faded rose, and a rusting washing machine on its side. A corner of the porch roof sagged down over one of a pair of windows flanking the front door—to Ruby it looked as if the house were sadly winking at her.

Ruby approached slowly, paused a good ten paces away from the house in the junk-strewn yard.

"Mr. Daniels!" she called, trying to keep a slight tremor from her voice. "I've come about the kohlrabi."

In a moment she heard a movement in the house, and then the door slowly opened.

Roland appeared in the doorway and peered out at her.

"It's Mrs. Glover, Mr. Daniels—I've come about the kohlrabi."

He moved out into the yard, still staring closely at her. He hardly seemed to recognize her, but then a smile creased his lips, grew, seemed to glow with the last light of the setting sun.

"It's sure nice of you to drop by," he said. He looked at the litter about him with a sad, embarrassed smile. "I don't keep things up like I used to—since my wife was gone—six years—1950 it was . . ."

Ruby felt sorry for the man. She'd never gotten over her Alexander, either. But she was also a little fidgety, dark being so near and still a mile between her and home.

"The kohlrabi, Mr. Daniels," she gently prodded.

"Oh. Yes."

He walked toward an old shed a few yards from the house and motioned her to follow. He paused before the door of the shed and stared off reflectively at the gold rim of the sky in the west. Lightening bugs winked at them from the woods.

"My wife used to like a mess of kohlrabi. I don't eat it myself—got no use for it—but I always grew a row or two for her in the garden. I don't know why I still grow it. Seems like a person has to do something for somebody other than hisself or there ain't no use in going on."

"It's getting late, Mr. Daniels. The kohlrabi?" she urged.

"Oh yes."

He stood a minute at the door, thinking, then he turned back to Ruby.

"Say, now, Mrs. Glover, here's a notion. Why don't you stay over for supper with me? I could fix us up some of that kohlrabi."

Ruby was stunned. It was almost dark, and she was a single woman, he a single man. What could he be thinking?

"Thank you, no," she finally managed to say. "I had my supper at the Workmans."

"Well, if you done already ate . . ."

He turned back to the shed, opened the door, then stood back and motioned her ahead. She stepped through the door into the gloom of the shed, so dark she could barely see the ears of corn rise in a slope from the floor of the shed near the door to half-way up the opposite wall. The smell of corn was thick and sweet in the air, but she saw no kohlrabi.

"Where—?"

She turned just as the door of the shed slammed in her face. She stood frozen in surprise and consternation as she heard Roland outside moving something heavy against the door, then a rasping noise as he wedged it in tight. She heard him walk away. She shoved at the door but could budge it only a fraction of an inch before Roland came back out of his house. He pushed the door all the way closed again, and then Ruby heard a click like a padlock being closed.

"Roland Daniels, what on earth!"

"I—I—I don't want you to be frightened a bit, Miss Glover, not a little bit. I wouldn't hurt a hair on your head or upset you in any way, but I just had to talk to you a bit."

"Why, I'll swan to John . . ."

"I just get lonely, Miss Glover. So lonely, and I know you do to. A body can't live without people, Miss Glover."

"Roland Daniels, you let me out of here this minute!"

"I tell you, Miss Glover, you're a fine woman, as

fine a woman as I've ever heard of."

"Mr. Daniels!"

"And I'll tell you another thing, I made myself a promise this year that I'd never go through another winter alone. Not one winter more."

"You're crazy as a hoot owl, Roland Daniels!"

It grew darker as he talked, and then it was as dark as that last night of spring would ever be. He talked gently and sadly of his loneliness, of living with a person you loved, and of the sorrows of living without that person. For a while Ruby would interrupt him with threats and commands and then pleas to open the door, but he just ignored her. So she announced that she was just going to sit there and not say a word or listen to a word until he came to his senses and let her out. Roland continued his somber litany of loneliness and need into the night. Only once did he stop and go into the house. Ruby heard pans banging around, and in a few minutes Roland came back and held a cup of steaming coffee through a paneless window high up on the wall of the shed. Ruby knocked it back out, and when Roland let out a "yelp" she muttered, "Serves you right." It was the last thing she said to him that night.

But it had no effect on Roland. He sat by the door whispering tenderly as the night hours passed, and as the morning neared he began to speak of his love for her. Ruby sat on the corn in silence and tried not to listen, but she heard every word.

At dawn Roland stopped and went back into the house, and Ruby heard the pots and pans banging again. In a little while he came back out and paused before the door. She could smell fried eggs, sausage, and coffee. He unlocked the padlock. Ruby stood back in the dark shadow of the corner of the shed, and when Roland stepped through the door with the dishes of food on a flat board, she hit him once over the head with a piece of two-by-four. He tottered and fell among the crashing dishes, pushed over onto his back with eyes rolling, said "catch the kitty" quite distinctly three times, and then lay still.

Ruby stepped over him and headed down the path that led to the Jerico road.

*

On a fine bright morning, the first day of July, Ruby was just finishing her house cleaning when she looked out the front door, started, and dropped her broom to the floor with a bang. Roland Daniels, wearing his old blue suit and new beige hat with the green band and dangling a paper sack in his right hand, ambled slowly across the footbridge and up to her house. Ruby moved a step back into the shadows but was too stunned to run out the back. Roland shuffled bashfully up to the door but didn't bother to knock. Through the screen he could see her in the shadows of the front room. He bowed his head penitently.

"Miss Glover, I come to apologize to you for the awful thing that I done."

Ruby's mouth worked but no words came.

"I'm a passionate man and a lonely man, but not a cruel man. I wouldn't hurt a fly, and I surely wouldn't hurt a hair on your head."

"Why you awful—" Her anger finally began to form itself around words.

"I come to—"

"I want you off of my property!"

"I just come to apologize, Miss Glover ma'am."

"Get out of my yard!"

"It was an awfull thing that I done, and I just wanted to apologize for it and leave off this mess of kohlrabi"—he held up the brown sack—"as a sort of a peace offering."

"I'll never touch it!"

"I've got lots more, and I could bring you a mess a couple times a week."

"You'll never!"

"Maybe I could bring you a bit every morning so you could have some with your noon dinner."

"Off my porch!"

"I'll just set this down here by the door, and maybe I'll just bring by another mess one day before the week's out."

"You'll never!"

Roland retreated across the footbridge and disappeared up the road. Ruby was livid. She opened the screen door and looked up the road both directions to make sure he was really gone. The sack of kohlrabi was at her feet. The gall of the man! Loneliness was one thing, but for his actions there was no excuse. She would have the law on him, maybe. But perhaps that was harsh. She'd ask Opal Workman for advice. Her husband, George, had as level a head as any in the area. She would think through this whole affair carefully and consider what would be best to do.

But first she hurried into the kitchen to put a pot of water on the stove. It'd been a long, long time since she'd cooked kohlrabi, but there wasn't much to it. Add a little salt—or sugar if you liked yours sweet—and throw in some bacon fat or a ham hock if you've got it. Then cook it long, cook it slow, cook it all the way down. It took a while, but—and her mouth watered at the thought—the wait was worth it.

WESLEY TUCKER'S "MISTERIOUS INDIAN BURIAL GROUNDS"

FOLKS NEVER DID THINK THAT Wesley Tucker treated poor Ida just right. He always had—well, not a wild streak exactly—but he flew off the handle easily and he was a big talker if not a doer and had one crazy harebrained scheme after another. Like the time he went to a movie—"God's Little Acre"—in Clinton and then took the notion to hitch-hike out to California to be a movie star just like the ugly old boy in that picture show. He left Ida alone out there on that farm for over seven weeks, but the women said that the worst thing he ever did to her was come back. When he did straggle back in finally, he'd lost a lot of weight—from the wild California women, he said with a wink, but folks figured it was just from starving—and he took pneumonia and was down for three more months, with poor Ida having to tend him and at the same time try to get what she could out of land that looked more like the remains of a rock quarry than a farm. And then he had the gall to survive the pneumonia, too. The women said that it was just like Wesley Tucker.

The California escapade wasn't the only grief that Wesley brought to Ida and probably wasn't even the worst—he seemed to get more flighty and lazy and cantankerous with age—but as the saying goes, if a man treating his wife poorly was a crime, wouldn't just niggers work chain gangs. What really set people against him was the way he acted after she died. He showed up at the funeral drunk and offered the bottle around and slapped men on the back and smoked a big old cigar he'd bought just for the occasion. After the few people who were there filed by the casket, they couldn't even get Wesley to go take a look. Acted like he didn't even recollect who was lying there and backed away from Robin's Song Carter, Ida's brother, when Robin's Song tried to lead him up the the casket to say good bye. Robin's Song looked real hurt, which is unusual because Indians normally don't show much feeling about anything. To top it off, after the ceremony they almost had to force Wesley to go out behind the church to the graveyard where they buried Ida, and when he finally did agree to go he just sat there on the folding chair and sulked and wouldn't look at anybody. Folks will forgive almost any kind of conduct to one in his sorrow, but Wesley Tucker hadn't shed a tear. And if a person is downright queer—like Rachel Mckutchern who lived by herself for years and years and then one day killed all her chickens and buried them in the front yard, each with a little cross made out of popsickle sticks on its tiny grave—well, they can look the other way for that, too.

But Wesley Tucker, he just wasn't showing respect for the dead.

The day after the funeral, Wesley disappeared completely. Folks thought, well, he's off again, and there were all kinds of rumors—Paris, South America, Hong Kong, Kansas City—but no one knew for sure. Two weeks later, however, word got around that the Tucker farm had been sold. A man in a suit came in a big car and behind him was a flatbed truck carrying a bulldozer hired out from Clinton. The dozer knocked down the house and barn and a couple of sheds, and three workmen got the remains in a pile and stared at it for a bit, but then left, and no one's seen them since.

Wesley Tucker came back a week later. He'd taken the money from the sale of the farm and bought an old house-trailer, silver in color and rusting, but not in terribly bad shape. The man he bought it from had pulled it down to Jerico, and there Wesley had paid Raymond Land's boy, Robert, three dollars to pull it on the rest of the way behind his pickup. Wesley had ridden back in the trailer the whole way but poked his head out the side window so he could see people as he passed. He had an expression on his face that was . . . well, folks couldn't agree on just what sort of expression it was.

No one knew where Wesley figured on parking the thing, but they weren't too surprised to hear that he'd hauled it onto a little hill way in the back of George Workman's farm. George was a good Christian soul and would treat any man as a friend and neighbor, even one as worthless as Wesley.

Wesley was a favorite topic of conversation for a

while, but he almost never came out of his trailer or hung around the Skelley station in Jerico like he used to, so folks kind of let him slip from their minds—that is, until some boys were hunting rabbits in the woods behind Workman's place and came up on the trailer and took a peak in the window just out of curiousity and saw Wesley and that woman. Folks were outraged—Ida not hardly cold in her grave yet.

The boys hadn't really gotten a good look at the woman, but the rumor spread that she was young and beautiful, and some type of foreigner, a gypsy or something like that. Wesley being past sixty and all, no one should have believed the young and beautiful part, but the wilder the rumor, the more folks are likely to believe it. That is, until those same boys went snooping around in the woods in back of Wesley Tucker's trailer again and ran right into the woman out picking greens. She looked at them real flat and mean-like—just like a copperhead, one of the boys said—and reached for something heavy in her pocket, so they lit out.

Although that part of the story was sort of exciting, the boys were disappointed on the whole, for the one thing that they agreed on was that she was not young and pretty. She was at least fifty, in fact, and she had thick legs and arms and a roll of fat like an inner-tube around her middle. And she had pulled her greasy black hair back from her forehead and let it fall in one long braid down her back, just like an Indian, they said. So folks said that she was an Indian. But George Workman said that she wasn't an Indian because she spoke with some sort of accent; he thought that she was a Mexican probably. That made sense because Sunday's Hollow had Indians of its own—the Carters and the Wallens—and they talked just like any white man; so people figured that Tucker's woman (in private she was called something not so delicate as that) was some sort of Mexican ("wetback," said Drew Stokes, who had been in the army).

Somehow, the word got back to Wesley that people were calling his woman a Mexican, and he flew off in a rage down the road through the Hollow to Jerico. He stopped everyone he met on the way and people on the street in Jerico and told them, "That woman out there's an *Indian*. I ain't living with no Mexican. Do you really think I'd stoop to lie with a Mexican woman?" The men just looked at him innocently like they'd never heard of any woman, then laughed fit to die when his back was turned. The women avoided him like something diseased, crossed to the other side of the street when he approached.

It was the first time that Wesley had been out in public since he had returned with the house-trailer. After he finished his rampage through town, he went back to the trailer, and no one saw him again for quite some time— except once when he charged out of the trailer with his double-barreled shotgun leveled at the boys, who wouldn't quit snooping around. The people of Sunday's Hollow prided themselves on their tolerance, but the shotgun episode convinced them that Wesley's behavior was becoming more than Christian folk could be expected to put up with. For George Workman's sake, if nothing else, something would have to be done because George was just too kind a man to drive Wesley off his property himself. Good as gold, George. Tucker's trailer had no water out there, and every morning George filled two five-gallon cans with water and carried them across the fields and up the hill to the trailer. And George older than Wesley and with a bad heart to boot. "Why George," said his sister, Mary Carter, "at least let that heathen carry his own water." But George just shrugged.

Sometimes a person can be simply too good for his own good.

The men had already begun to gather and speak vaguely of a certain "visit" they were liable to have to make before long, when one day Wesley saved them all the trouble. David Don Stokes had just left Workman's house after a visit with George when he saw a fat woman with a floppy red dress and no shoes on running across the field, followed about ten yards behind by Wesley Tucker. They weren't running exactly since both were a little old for that, but they were stepping right out, and every few yards the woman, who was keeping up a surprisingly good pace despite her bulk, would look back over her shoulder and adjust her speed to stay ahead of Wesley. And closer up David Don saw why, for high up above Wesley's head, like a torch raised in a furious procession, gleamed a wicked-looking corn knife. David Don sped up to try to intercept them—actually started running, which was no small feat since he had long ago passed his first half-century himself and had that gimpy leg on top of it—and caught Wesley from behind just as he hit the road. They struggled over the knife for a couple of minutes while Wesley cussed and raged and begged to be let at that "wetback bitch" until David Don saw that the woman had padded safely out of sight up over the hill, and then deciding that neither she nor Wesley was worth much of his blood anyway, he loosed his hold on Wesley and backed quickly away like he had just lit a short fuse on a big firecracker. Wesley wheezed and panted and glared up the hill and then back at David Don, but didn't say a word, just turned with the corn knife still clutched in his fist and stalked off in the direction of his trailer.

No one ever found out what the fuss had been about—people of that ilk just naturally aren't meant to live with another—and no one ever figured out how that woman got out of the Hollow and through Jerico without anyone seeing her, but at least they were rid of her, for good, apparently. George Workman said that she never came back to the trailer, and George Workman was not a man to tell a lie, so that settled that.

People guessed that now Wesley would make a hermit out of himself back there in that trailer, but they were wrong. The very next day he was seen rummaging about through the woods and in ditches along the road, around abandoned homesteads and along creek banks. He carried a small old cardboard suitcase, and every once in a while he'd spot something among the rocks and bend over and lay his suitcase down and open it and put the article inside. People would ask him what it was that he was collecting, but he'd just hug the suitcase close to his chest and peer back suspiciously. His hair was growing long and grey under the sweat-stained straw hat perched on top of his head, and although he had never before let his whiskers grow, he now wore a beard. He spoke to no one. People thought that now he was "touched," had been, perhaps, all along, and because of it they treated him with a new deference. One old gossip suggested that this was the result of the despicable, maddening disease that often afflicted those men who trafficked with a woman such as the Mexican, but the people of the Hollow would have none of it. They could forgive a man anything who had been driven to the brink by his troubles.

After about a month of this behavior, Wesley gave the people of the Hollow something else to think about. One day they found that his trailer had been moved from George Workman's farm over to Francis Oates' place, right behind his house in fact. "Dang, Francis, are you letting that crazy old coot live right in your back yard?" they asked him. "Nope," he replied smuggly, "that trailer's mine now."

It seems that Wesley had traded Oates his trailer for the deed to about four acres of worthless land that ran along side the road about a quarter of a mile from Oates' house. A few people were a little indignant at Oates, taking advantage of a poor old geezer that didn't have enough sense to pour piss out of a boot, and Oates got about half hot defending himself. Said it was Tucker who wanted to make the deal, insisted on it, and that business was business. A fool and his money and all that.

If anyone thought that the trade was unfair, it certainly wasn't Wesley. He seemed happy as a lark, working about the place day and night, but nobody could figure out what he was doing. First he staked off the land, driving short spikes of wood into the ground around the perimenter and tying old pieces of cloth to them, almost like a surveyor. Then he set about clearing some of the smaller trees and brush with an old ax and shovel that Oates had thrown into the deal (he also kicked in an extra 150 bucks, but whether this was originally part of the bargain or whether later he had added it because of guilt and public scorn, no one could say). After knocking some saplings down and cutting a little brush, Wesley hauled some boards out of the trash that was still piled up on his old farm and built a small shack, not much bigger than an outhouse. Winter was a long way off yet, and people thought that he could at least get some shelter from the rain there. He didn't stop with the shack, though. He bought a roll of baling wire from Oates (almost *gave* it to the old guy, Oates said) and strung the wire between trees all the way around the perimeter of his land, then tied red bits of cloth to the wire and collected the stakes. For the next week or so Wesley split most of his time between working on another shack and chasing away anyone who got within cussing distance. One Saturday he went into Riney's store in Jerico and bought up a bunch of paint, dyes, cheap cloth, string, glue, and other assorted items, and then spent almost another full week inside one or another of the shacks. He was working away on something, but no one could say what, and no one dared get too close; he could still let fly with a rock pretty good for an old boy.

That Saturday Francis Oates drove into Jerico and pulled up beside the Skelley station that the farmers were in the habit of loafing around when they came into town. There were already a half-dozen lolling around swapping lies when Oates strolled up with his thumbs hooked in his overall straps and a sassy grin on his face and said, "What're you boys doing in town? You're missing the show."

"What show?" they shot back.

"What show? Why, Wesley Tucker's show, that's what show. What-in-the-hell other show would I be talking about?"

The men looked at one another quizzically.

"What do you think he's been working on out there all this time?" Oates said.

"That's what we're asking you."

"Well, it's a genuine 'Indian Burial Grounds,' that's what it is."

"What the Sam Hell are you talking about—'Indian Burial Grounds'?"

Oates shrugged. "I dunno. Go out there and pay your quarter and see."

"Pay! You mean he's charging for one of his bullshit wingdings?"

"I tell you what. You try to get in there without paying a quarter and see how fast you get beaned. He may even have that old shotgun of his in one of those shacks."

Of course, they all went out there to see, and it was no time before the rest of the people in Jerico and Sunday's Hollow had heard about it. Everyone said that it was about as good a way to waste a quarter as throwing it in the river, but they went anyway. Old Wesley had dyed some turkey feathers red and yellow and blue and pasted them on a strip of cloth and tied it around his head for a headdress. (I ain't no Injun," he said emphatically, "I'm just getting folks in the mood.") He'd taken the rest of the dyed feathers and hung them from the wire that bordered the grounds. He also hung at intervals some old sheets that he'd dyed and painted to look like what he imagined an Indian blanket would look like. As a gate in the wire he fixed a two-by-four on a hinge to a tree so that he could open it or swing it shut and hook it to a nail in the tree opposite. He kept a pocketful of rocks and a wary eye out in case anyone ventured too close to the grounds without paying. Just over the gate hung a two-by-eight on which Wesley had painted "Indian Burial Grounds." After the first couple of days he replaced this one with a fancier sign, the letters stenciled on in alternating red and white—"Wesley Tucker's 'Misterious Indian Burial Grounds'." On a table just inside the gate were rows of arrow- and spearheads, obviously what Wesley had been collecting for the last month or so. The small ones could be purchased for a quarter each and the larger ones for 50 cents. Everyone around Sunday's Hollow had coffee cans filled with arrowheads, of course, so business was not too good. The "Indian blankets" he priced at $10 each. In the little shack was where Wesley lived, but in the slightly larger shack was indeed a startling sight—the remains of a human skeleton laid out on an Indian blanket-draped table. Wesley said that that was the remains of the famous Osage chief, King Homatoo. No one could recall any King Homatoo, but Wesley swore it was so and offered as proof the skull, upon which was carved, quite neatly in block letters, KING HOMATOO, OSAGE CHIEF.

"You know," he explained, eyes flashing wildly about, "that was the custom—to carve their names on their foreheads so the gods would know them . . . that's a fact."

Naturally a person couldn't do anything but agree, and at first everybody about laughed themselves into the hospital. Later, though, several people got a little suspicious about the origin of that for-sure real skeleton, and some even went to graveyards to check, but none had been tampered with, and no one in the area was reported missing. No one ever found out where the skeleton came from, but some guessed that maybe Wesley had in fact stumbled onto the remains of some Indian or early settler.

But Wesley didn't claim that there was just one skeleton; he swore that his entire property was riddled with graves of Indian dead. He said that he dared not disturb any more of the graves or the curse would come down upon his head. "What curse?" someone asked him. "Death alone," he said. Now what in blazes did that mean? "A lot of folks die alone," Francis Oates snorted. "What's so special about that?" Nobody spent a lot of time on it, though. There might be two or three greater wastes of time than trying to inspect one of Wesley Tucker's wild hairs, but no one had run across them yet.

Still, even though Wesley refused to do any more digging, he didn't figure walking around a little on them would disturb the dead too much, and so a tour was offered with the two-bit admission price—the highlight of the whole attraction. Wesley would lead the way with an old metal pants press stretched out in front of him at arm's length and parallel to the ground. Hanging from a string tied to the far end of the press was a bone which Wesley claimed was from the right index finger of King Homatoo. He said that when he crossed over a grave the bone would pull the press down, point out the King's tribesmen, as Wesley put it.

He'd even let the customer lay his hand along the press, and then he'd stop periodically and say, "There! There! Feel that? Don't you feel the King pointing the way?"

And of course everyone agreed that they felt it.

The funny thing was that Wesley really seemed to believe his own story. He'd get furious if someone so much as hinted that the sheets and blankets and turkey feathers that he'd painted up himself weren't authentic.

Wesley had a pretty good business going for a while. Everyone in the area seemed to feel that it was almost an obligation to pay Wesley his quarter and take the tour, but no one was crazy enough to do it more than once. So after a couple of weeks, Wesley just sort of piddled around, adjusting a blanket here or there, chasing off some smart-alecky kids, or gathering more arrowheads that he hadn't managed to sell a one of.

But then a curious thing happened. One Sunday a young man in a white shirt and tie and sunglasses drove into Jerico and asked where he could find Mr. Wesley Tucker and his Indian burial grounds. He said that he was a reporter for the *Kansas City Star*, and he wanted to take a few pictures. They told him at the Skelley station how to get there. Then the word spread fast, and soon half the town and most of the Hollow were over at the grounds again. The reporter talked to Wesley for a good while and took the tour, put his hands on the pants press, and even took several pictures, just like he said he would. Then he went to his car and wrote some notes down in a little book and tried to talk to some of the bystanders, but most were too shy to admit that they knew anything about it, although several offered a little sheepishly that Wesley was one or two bricks shy of a load. The reporter smiled at that and drove off.

Two weeks later, sure enough, there was an article on one of the back pages of the Sunday *Star*. George Workman's sister Ella sent it to him from Sedalia. It had two pictures, one of the whole grounds with the blankets and feathers and everything and another of Wesley himself looking stern and dedicated in the headdress and holding the pants press up to his shoulder like a soldier at attention. The article was kind of tongue-in-cheek, but it never did come right out and say that Wesley wasn't playing with a full deck. There wasn't just a flood of visitors after that, but for about a month people came in fairly steadily from as far away as Clinton and Sedalia and even Kansas City. Even some of the local people paid to get in a second time, though if anyone accused them of it they would deny it on their mothers' honor.

Wesley seemed happy as could be, was even making a little money on the deal, but after about a month or so it all started to die down again. After a while he was lucky to get a couple of curious souls on the weekend, and then even that stopped. He gathered more arrowheads, took down some blankets and put up others, and painted King Homatoo's shack to look more presentable, but no one came. Finally the people of the Hollow wouldn't even glance over in his direction when they passed. He seemed to disappear for a few days, but then he was back, and before long he had a new attraction.

King Homatoo had been shunted off to a box that was so small the bones were just piled on top of one another, and on his shack was now a sign saying, "Princess Warmheart—$10." Wesley didn't advertise his new attraction too much, not openly at least. He let Francis Oates in for free and told him that if there was anything in there that he thought anybody else might care for, he might pass the word. And that's what Oates did, and soon Wesley's business was healthier than ever.

Except that it had taken a curiously nocturnal turn—he wouldn't even let anyone in in the daytime—and the customers were strictly men, young men mostly at that.

Unfortunately for Wesley, goings on like that just cannot be hushed up in a close community like the Hollow. Mrs. Oates was one of the first to get suspicious—Francis spent entirely too much time down there, and why always at night? Soon rumors were flying. Two school boys claimed to have snuck up to Tucker's shack early one morning and to have seen that same Mexican woman that had lived with Wesley before. The widow Turnbull corroborated the story, saying she'd seen the Mexican strolling through the woods one day with a beer can in her hand! People refused to speculate openly about what kind of business Tucker was running—such knowledge should not be at a decent person's command!—but they whispered it enough privately, and after church one Sunday night Reverend Greene held a private meeting of the menfolk. Afterwards the men—two dozen of them—marched up the road to Tucker's and hollered for him and his whore to come out.

Wesley came out all right, shotgun leveled and ready to do damage, but they were prepared. Three men had already crept up on the shack. One grabbed the shotgun from behind and another slugged Wesley on the side of the jaw. Wesley fell like an empty sack. He sat there dazed and spitting blood from the cut in his mouth and listened without much interest, apparently, to the wires twanging as they were cut away from the trees with axes. They hauled the Mexican woman out of the shack and stuffed her in a car and drove her to the county line to dump her ("kickin' and screamin' and bitin' and cussin' in

Mexican and English and six other languages it sounded like," said Ferris McCrady). They knocked down the signs and grabbed as many blankets and feathers as they could find and threw them in the shack, poured gasoline inside, and set it afire. They went into the other shack and grabbed up some of Wesley's pots and pans and clothes and stuff so that he wouldn't be left with nothing, then set that shack on fire, too. Before they left they formed a circle around Wesley, who was still too dazed to move, and the Reverend bent down close and hissed, "Get out of the county, Tucker. We're done fed up. Be gone by tomorrow."

As they left, one of them gave the table filled with arrowheads a kick and stones flew off into the night in all directions.

*

Wesley sat there on the ground while the voices trooped off up the road, and he sat there for a long time after they had completely died away. The shacks were still burning at his back, so he was not cold, but his head buzzed and ached and he was still dizzy. After an hour or so, he crawled over to a tree and sat with his back against it and watched the flames licking at the black heart of the night. He watched until the flames died down, flickered, vanished, then saw the wind blow the glowing ashes into golden whirls of sparks like tangled clouds of fiery gnats. By the time the dawn crawled up through the trees on his left, he had not closed his eyes once. He sat watching the smoldering ashes of the shacks. He shivered from the cold and ached all over now, and his cheek felt like he had bitten a hole in it. He couldn't spit out the strong metallic taste of blood.

He felt very old.

The Reverend had told him to get out of the county on this day. He supposed that he had better try to go somewhere, but he didn't have anyplace to go. A low fog lurked about the trunks of the trees up the road. The road would take him to Jerico, but it was a long walk, and he didn't feel up to it. Besides, he would almost certainly meet someone on the way, and that might not be too good. He might get Francis Oates to drive him on out of the county, but he couldn't even bring himself to try to stand up. He felt very old.

He longed for Ida.

OLD SOLDIER

WHEN HE AWOKE TO THE SCREAM in the night, he first imagined that he was back in Nam. Then, when he realized he was in his own bed in Jerico, he thought that he must have been dreaming. Except that he didn't dream of Vietnam.

Sometimes it bothered him, that he did not dream of war. He wondered if he was not quite normal, like a person who didn't mind having a tooth pulled. But then he wasn't like everyone else. Not everyone had seen combat in three wars. If he'd wanted to dream, there'd been plenty to dream about.

He'd gotten out two years after Tet with twenty-nine years on his sleeve. He hadn't waited for the one more year; he didn't need the money. But it wasn't fear that drove him out. He couldn't remembered the last time he'd been afraid. Not in Nam. Korea? He'd been cold in Korea, he remembered cold, but fear? No. Maybe at the

Bulge. Yes, he'd been afraid at the Bulge, although it was no worse than Korea, after the Chinese came with their bugles in the night, no worse than Vietnam, where the soldiers were so young—boys really—crying over their M-16s.

If he'd wanted to dream, he could have dreamed about Jeffries, who'd hollered down the trail to them that night after the ambush, *Please God help me I'm hurt Please God help me I'm hurt* over and over until his men wept and pleaded to be allowed to attack back up the trail, and the fairy ROTC Second Lieutenant stood there trembling and white-faced, unable to say a word, and the soldier had said *No, no one goes back* and sat down in the middle of the trail with the .50 caliber machine gun in his lap and said he'd shoot anyone who tried to get past him. And they knew he would do it. He sat there all night while they cursed and threatened him, until Jeffries stopped screaming. They never said a word to him after that, said nothing, as if they thought that'd bother him. A First Sergeant didn't have friends. The only one who'd said anything to him was Lt. Abbot. "You know," he'd said in that weak-kneed, hang-dog way of his, "I know you were right about not going back for Jeffries, but the thing is, I've got a little boy, Greg, three years old, and I kept thinking, what if that'd been Greg up there? Jeffries was somebody's son. What if he'd been mine? You know what I mean?"

"No," the soldier had said.

"I've got a hundred and sixty babies to take care of right here," he'd joke of his company whenever somebody asked him about a family. He had no family outside the army, didn't want one because he didn't know what he was missing, if anything. He figured he'd experienced more in three wars than a dozen family men, civilians, could dream of. That life he didn't lead outside the army, well, it was like dreams of war. He didn't have them, so they didn't touch him.

The truth was, war bored him, and that, not fear, was why he'd gotten out of the army, worked for two years for the post office in Kansas City, gotten bored there, too. So he pitched it all and moved to Jerico, a little town on the northwest edge of the Ozarks where, he had to remind himself, he'd been born and lived with his father before running off to join the army at seventeen.

He couldn't remember the house they'd lived in. Maybe it still existed; maybe not. It didn't interest him. In seventeen years he must have made a friend or two, but he couldn't conjure up a face, event, or anecdote. Although occasionally a last name overheard down at the Git-n-Go, where he gassed up the car and bought milk and bread, would ring a distant bell, he couldn't swear that he remembered a single individual in Jerico. He remembered a one-room school with a pot-bellied stove at the front next to the teacher's desk. One winter day he was punished by being made to sit in the corner in the back, where he got so cold that he cried. But he couldn't remember what he'd done wrong. He remembered straining to keep up with his father in the pre-dawn darkness, day after day, on the path that led to the farm his father rented outside of town. He remembered his father's rough hands, but not his voice. He thought that, if he tried hard enough, he might remember his face. But he didn't try. The soldier had been barely fifty miles away, at Ft. Leonard Wood, when word came of his father's death, but he hadn't returned for the funeral. "My family's here," he'd told the C. O.

No, he hadn't come back to Jerico because of memories or family. He had few of one and none of the other. He had to retire somewhere, that was all, and he had an image of Jerico as a place where he could be by himself for once in his life, where people minded their own business and he'd mind his. And it didn't hurt that the Lake of the Ozarks wasn't far away, so he could fish there or in the creek that cut through the timber a hundred yards in back of his house. He hadn't been there long, though, before he found that he was spending most of his time listening to the radio or reading a newspaper—but not finding anything new.

*

He was fully awake now. He wasn't thinking about Vietnam; he was thinking about the scream. It had not been a dream. He lay still, listening to his own monotonous breathing. Suddenly, a sound from the house thirty yards to the east. A door opening. Someone walking across the back yard. The squeaking of the outhouse door swinging open and then closed. Two heavy thumps. Someone walking back across the yard.

He leaned up in bed and looked out the window in time to see the young woman walk onto her back porch and into the house. She wore a heavy man's coat over a long flannel nightgown.

He looked back at the outhouse. Something was different about it, something wrong, but he couldn't make it out, even though the moon lit up the landscape like a white phosphorous shell.

He stared a long time before he noticed the piece of wood wedged tight in the outhouse door.

*

He got up just after dawn the next morning and got his fishing gear ready. A bass would taste mighty good for breakfast. But instead of hiking on down to the creek, the soldier sat down at the kitchen table and sipped at a cup of coffee. It would be damn cold on the creek. Besides, he'd fished every day his first two or three weeks in Jerico, and—he had to admit it—he was getting bored with it.

Boredom disturbed him. He had retired young; he was still only fifty-three, and the rest of his life seemed like a broad valley still to cross, mined and booby-trapped with boredom.

He walked over to the kitchen window and looked across the gully to the house next door—back porch, back yard, pump, clothesline, outhouse. The piece of wood was gone from the outhouse door.

He ate breakfast and washed the dishes and was almost finished reading the *Clinton Eye* when he heard sounds next door.

The little boy—he couldn't have been over five or six—was playing in the back yard. He looked frail and chalky white and wore only a denim jacket against the bright cold February morning. The boy had a long stick that he was using as a rifle. He pointed it at the outhouse and went "Pow!" at his house "Pow!" at the birds "Pow!" He pointed it across the gully at the soldier's house and went "Pow!" The soldier retreated from the window.

When he finished the newspaper and glanced out the window again, the boy was no longer playing with the stick. He was sitting on a tree stump using a screwdriver to gouge off pieces of bark. His breath hovered about him like white smoke.

Then the soldier noticed the boy's face—the left side. It seemed to be covered with dirt or soot. No, it wasn't dirt, but the soldier couldn't quite tell . . .

He dug his binoculars out of the closet. The officers' field glasses were among only a few things—a field jacket and liner, a bayonet and scabbard, and a Colt .45 pistol—that he had taken with him when he retired. He could have made off with any number of things—he was a First Sergeant, after all—but he took only what he could use. He wasn't the type to collect souvenirs; he had no need for remembrance.

He lifted the binoculars, zeroed in on the boy, adjusted the focus. He sucked his breath in in a hiss, tried to steady his hands on the glasses. It wasn't dirt on the boy's face, not soot. A swollen bruise of purple and black ran from his eyebrow across the cheekbone and ended in a puff of green and red on his jaw. The bruise flashed stark and ghastly against his pale skin and hair like the clotted-blood heart of a white gauze wound dressing.

*

It might have been an accident. More likely, the kid's old man had busted him one. The soldier would see the father leaving or arriving in his rusty Ford pickup. He was young, looked barely draft age, and always had on grease-stained Levis, boots caked with grease, hands black and hair matted with it. The soldier thought that he must work in one of the gas stations in Warsaw. The soldier had been outside the house a couple of times when the young man was working on his pickup, not twenty yards away, but he'd not once looked the soldier in the eye. He had a tough, sullen air. The soldier had seen many of his kind in basic training, and he'd broken them fast.

If he thought about it too much, he'd get angry, but he knew it was none of his business Besides, the kid probably deserved it. He looked like a wild one for sure, and the discipline always has to be one step tougher than the kid. Has to. He'd broken a couple of noses, loosened a few teeth himself when he was an SDI in the basic training battalion at Ft. Leonard Wood. Take a kid who thought he was going to have it his way, get him off to himself, and work him over. Get the other sergeants to say he attacked you. You had to do it, and it worked. In the long run, it was for the kid's own good.

But the boy next door was so little, so pale.

*

Two days later the soldier was fishing on the creek when the boy came out of the bushes and stared silently down at the brown, turgid water. The bruise was a deep charcoal, fading to rose, green, and yellow at the edges.

"Hi, sonny. Got yourself a shiner there, looks like." The boy stared at the water. The soldier tried to think of something to say. He didn't have much experience with children.

"You won't catch no fish."

The boy had said it so suddenly, so softly, that the soldier wasn't sure he heard him right.

Then the boy turned and disappeared back into the woods.

Afterward, without intending for it to happen, the soldier found himself standing watch at the kitchen window, hours at a time.

*

It was less than a week after he saw the boy at the creek that the soldier heard a commotion next door. He got to the window just as the mother caught the little boy by the stump in their back yard, jerked his pants down, and began to beat him with a section of clothesline. The soldier went into the living room and turned on the radio. He found a country and western station, then turned the volume up.

But he could still hear the clothesline, singing in the air.

*

The soldier would stand at the window and watch the woman next door. He had seen her kind in the enlisted men's housing on every army post in the world. They married young and saw the possibilities close off one by one. Haggard. Harried. Exhausted. Ferocious. You would not stand between one and a bargain table at a store. They were direct as an anti-tank rocket. Before they were thirty, their breasts began to sag, flesh gathered at the waist, at the ankles, in rings at the neck.

He would stare out at the woman and think lovingly of the Colt .45 on the shelf in the closet.

But no, the pistol stayed right where it was. He was retired from war. Besides, you don't go back up the trail at night, not after Jeffries or anyone else. You don't go back up the trail unless the gain is worth the risk. Here, he stood to gain nothing because he had nothing invested. It wasn't his battle.

*

He began to spend more time in Warsaw, the resort town a dozen miles up the blacktop on the other side of Sunday's Hollow. He had no particular reason to be there—he wasn't seeking the society of men, that was for sure—but in Warsaw was about the only time he could drag himself away from the window. Gradually, he began to spend almost all day there.

But that didn't take care of the night.

It was near the end of February when he heard the scream again, lurched up in bed and then, groggy, looked out the window. The woman was dragging the boy across the back yard. She slung him inside the outhouse and slammed the door, wedged a piece of wood in the door and fixed it in place with two thumps of the heel of her hand.

The soldier felt a pain in his hands and looked down. He had been digging his nails into the windowsill, and splinters and bits of old varnish were jammed under them. He pressed his fingertips against the window, and soon the cold numbed away the pain.

Frost bloomed in a circle when he breathed on the

window. How long could the boy live in a cold, drafty outhouse? He opened the window all the way to prove to himself how much the cold hurt. He shivered and wrapped a blanket about himself. At the Bulge, the snow had been littered with black nuggets: fingers and toes frozen brittle and snapped off. *That* was cold. That was much worse than this. *Much* worse than this. That was much worse . . .

He promised himself that if the boy wasn't released by midnight, he'd march right over there, come hell or high water.

No. It was not his battle. You do not go back up the trail at night. You do not go back after Jeffries. How he had screamed! *Please God help me I'm hurt!* And the boy wasn't screaming, not even making a sound, so he would not go back up the trail. He would sit by the window, but that's all that can be expected of you if you're retired from war.

*

He did his best to stand guard by the window, but even with the cold and uncomfortable posture, he felt himself nodding off. Suddenly, he was dreaming. Not of Nam, and not of the boy. He dreamt of Kansas City and a fellow postal worker named Russell who had invited him to dinner. Russell and his wife and children—there must have been a dozen of them—treated him so nicely, were so attentive, offering him the best of the food and taking nothing for themselves. And right as the dream ended Russell asked him—almost sorrowfully, it seemed—"Don't you ever regret it, the other life?" "What other life?" the soldier had just started to ask when the dream ended.

It had been a funny dream because he didn't have a friend named Russell in Kansas City. He'd made no friends in Kansas City at all.

When he awoke from the dream, false dawn was brightening the sky, and the outhouse door was ajar.

*

The next afternoon the woman started in on the boy again. First there was screaming from the house, then the back door flew open and the boy ran out into the yard, followed closely by the mother waving a black leather belt high over her head.

The soldier found himself running out the back of his house and up to the gully that separated his property from his neighbors.

At the edge of the gully he stopped, and at the same instant the woman saw him and stopped running, the belt still help high over her head, face twisted in surprise, fear, and outrage.

"Only a boy . . ." was all the soldier could manage to say.

The woman's mouth worked for a moment before sound came.

"You mind your own business!"

"It'll be my business if you hit that boy again."

Suddenly the woman turned and grabbed the boy and ran with him back to the house.

She paused at the porch door and, tears now streaming down her face, screamed at the soldier, "I'm calling Eddie! You'll learn to mind your business once my

Eddie gets home!"

She disappeard into the house with the boy, and the soldier ran around to the front of his house and climbed into his old Dodge and headed for Warsaw.

On the short drive to Warsaw, all the soldier could think of was *Maybe I should have gone back up the trail, maybe . . .*

But what would there have been to gain? And what lose? A life, maybe. His life. And what was that?

*

Sheriff Naylor wasn't anxious to get involved. "These family squabbles are a pain in the ass to get messed up in." Finally the sheriff had called old George Workman, who knew about everyone in Sunday's Hollow and Jerico, and after talking to George a few minutes, the sheriff had sighed and said, "Let's go."

*

Sheriff Naylor followed the soldier to Jerico in his station wagon. By the time they got there, the husband's pickup was out front. The sheriff, with the soldier right behind, was about halfway up the stone steps leading from the bottom of the ditch to the house when the front door came open just enough to allow the long black barrel of a rifle to slide out at them.

"Guess I'm gonna have to kill a few people you come on my property, sheriff," came the voice of the young man.

"Wouldn't think of it," the sheriff said, holding his

palms up placatingly and backing slowly down the steps.

By the end of this brief conversation, the soldier was face down in the ditch. He was retired, but he had been in three wars and he knew what to do when a rifle barrel aimed in his direction.

"Sir, I think you can come up out of there," the sheriff said. "Eddie ain't going to shoot anybody."

The soldier got up on all fours, but didn't come up out of the ditch. The sheriff walked around his car so that it was between him and the house.

"OK," he called toward the house, "I'm off your property now, Eddie. Can we talk?"

The house was silent for a moment, then Eddie's voice came out: "Looks like some son-of-a-bitch already been doing some talking. Some outsider come in here, not even one of us, and tries to tell us how to run our business."

The soldier leaned over against the slope, inched up so that he could just see the rifle barrel, which was pointing more in the sheriff's direction than his.

"You're probably right, Eddie. That's why I'd like to come in there alone, just me, and talk to you about your boy."

"My son's my business. Ain't nobody else's."

The sheriff shook his head.

"Not if there's harm being done to him, Eddie. Then it's my business."

"Is that what that liar told you?"

The soldier saw the rifle barrel dip, train down toward the ditch.

"He's a lying bastard if he said that!"

"That's what I figured, Eddie. That's why I figured

if you'd let me come in there and talk with you and the missus and the boy . . ."

Eddie's voice came out low and soft so that the soldier could barely hear: "Well, I guess I might have to shoot you after all, sheriff."

"No, you won't have to do that."

"The law starts sticking its nose in—I know where that goes. Looks like I'll have to shoot you and the son-of-a-bitch with you, then I'll have to shoot the boy, cause I ain't letting nobody come take him away from me."

"You don't have to do that, Eddie."

"Looks like it."

"No, you don't."

The soldier saw the rifle barrel jump and then the blast shook the air. The soldier threw himself down into the bottom of the ditch and looked over toward the sheriff. He didn't see him at first, but then he saw him on the ground staring wildly at him from under the car and pointing up the road toward the soldier's house. He looked scared but unhurt. Eddie was either a very bad shot or had fired into the air.

The soldier did the lowcrawl up the ditch toward his house, then heard the door of the sheriff's car open and the engine starting. The soldier turned and watched the car roll slowly toward him, the sheriff's head bobbing up above the dash every few seconds. The car rolled past him and on up the road and didn't stop until, the soldier guessed, his house was between the sheriff and Eddie.

The soldier had forgotten how exhausting the low-crawl was. By the time he made it up the ditch to the deeper gully, then did the duck walk up the gully until he was out of the field of fire beyond his house, he was wheezing and drenched with sweat.

But he felt good. He felt excited. He was back on home ground, he was back in war, and this one wasn't Korea or Vietnam, a war for nothing, this one was for a little boy, the son, he suddenly realized, he might have had in a different life.

He climbed up out of the gully and walked over to the sheriff's car.

"Close call," the soldier said.

Sheriff Naylor shrugged. He seemed to have calmed down.

"Aw, he wasn't trying to hit me. I'd've been dead if that'd been it. He's just trying to show us that he's getting into a fairly serious mood about things."

"Maybe. Well, what're we going to do?"

"*We* ain't going to do nothing. You're going to stay out of the way and let me handle this. I'm going to get ahold of the State Police. I hate to bring them in because that'll mean big trouble for the boy, but you just can't go around squeezing off rounds at duly elected law enforcement officials."

Sheriff Naylor picked up the mike from his CB and cleared his throat.

"I've got a .45 in the house," the soldier said.

The sheriff set the mike down.

"And that's just where it's going to stay—in the house."

He picked the mike up again and started to speak.

"I've seen these situations a hundred times in the army," the soldier said. "You rush them fast and you can catch them off guard. Let them stay in there awhile and think about it, all kinds of bad things can happen."

The sheriff threw the mike down on the seat.

"Now you're starting to get me all varieties of pissed. You don't stay out of things, I'm gonna handcuff your ass to the car! . . . Now, I don't like to talk like that, but you got to let trained law enforcement personnel handle these things, that's all."

Civilians. Let civilians run things and you'll have something then, all right, the soldier thought. Sheriff Naylor was a nice enough fellow, but probably the most dangerous situation he'd dealt with was little boy's throwing cherry bombs on the 4th of July. In a crisis somebody with experience has to take charge. Three wars had taught the soldier that.

The soldier stepped down into the gully, going in the direction of his house. He heard the CB pop and hiss, then the sheriff's voice. Instead of crossing the gully, however, the soldier turned left and headed in the direction of the young couple's house. He walked bent over, and then was down on all fours where the gully met the ditch. It wasn't until then, apparently, that Sheriff Naylor realized what was going on, for just as the soldier was about to follow the sharp right turn of the gully between the two houses, he heard the sheriff's furious hiss:

"What the hey! You damn fool, get back here! That's a blinking order! . . . Well I'll be eternally goddamn."

The gully was wider but shallower between the houses, and the soldier had to half-crawl, half-slither along. By the time he came opposite the back door of the couple's house, he was gulping fire and bleeding at the palms, elbows, and knees. He turned and looked back down the gully, but the sheriff was nowhere to be seen.

He would go in through the back. Eddie couldn't

watch the back and front at once. If he had his wife post-
ed as a guard, the soldier would be in big trouble, he
knew that, but he figured he could count on civilians not
to think things through. Even if no one was watching the
back, though, it would be almost impossible for him to
get into the house and get the boy out unless the sheriff
was smart enough to provide some distraction up front.
There was no telling what would happen, but the soldier
thought that by forcing things he might make the sheriff
grow into the situation, be better than he could be. The
soldier had seen it happen in war before. Anyway, in the
crisis of battle, whoever took charge had to make the best
decision he could given what he knew at the time, then
go with it and not look back.

The soldier came up out of the gully and charged
the house. For two or three exhilarating seconds he was
exposed, naked, but then he was crouching behind the
screen door of the back porch. No one was on the porch,
but there was a glare on the window of the door that led
into the house, and the soldier couldn't see in.

He had just touched the handle of the door when
he heard a car starting up, then slowly approaching the
house. Sheriff Naylor. Good boy.

The soldier pulled open the screen door and
stepped onto the porch. He eased up to the door that led
into the house, put an eye to one corner of the window,
and cupped his hand against the glare.

He was looking into the kitchen. Across the
kitchen was a door that led into the living room. In the
living room, silhouetted against the light of the front
door window, stood Eddie, the rifle pointed out toward
the road.

At that moment he heard Sheriff Naylor's voice coming from the road. He started to listen but suddenly saw, huddled in the corner of the kitchen, the boy.

The soldier tried the doorknob, found it unlocked. Carefully, he opened the door a crack. The boy swung his huge eyes toward him. The soldier motioned for him to come. The boy didn't move. The soldier eased the door open a bit more, took a step inside. Eddie was still at the front door, listening to the sheriff. The mother was nowhere to be seen. The soldier motioned to the boy. The boy pressed himself back into the corner. The soldier stepped on into the room. Took another step. Motioned to the boy. Took another step. Motioned to the boy. The boy stared back. The soldier took another step, was now out of Eddie's line of vision.

"Come to me," he mouthed silently.

The boy stared.

Now the soldier was standing over the boy. He knelt.

"Come with me, sonny."

The boy shook his head.

The soldier held out his hand, touched the boy's hand. The boy jerked his hand back. The soldier grabbed him by the wrist and yanked him across the floor.

"No!" the boy screamed.

The soldier pulled him, now opposite the kitchen door. Slowly, Eddie turned away from the front door, stared at the soldier.

"Come on, son!"

"No!"

Eddie pulled the rifle barrel out of the crack of the door, swung it around toward the soldier.

"Mama!"

Suddenly, the door was filled with the mother, coming at him.

"Mama!" screamed the boy, pulling against the soldier.

"Get out of the damn way, Terri!" Eddie shouted.

—Terri jumping back out of the doorway—Eddie aiming, then falling to the side as the door bursts open—Sheriff Naylor and Eddie struggling with the rifle—"Mama!"—the mother back in the doorway coming for the soldier who finds himself down on the floor rolling in pain clutching his groin—the boy free, hugging his mother around the legs and screaming "Mama! Mama!"—

*

The soldier was sitting on his couch, his knees pulled up almost under his chin. His privates throbbed painfully.

Sheriff Naylor, sitting opposite him, smiled wrily.

"That little bugger kicked you a good one, didn't he?"

The soldier shook his head.

"I just can't figure it out. I was trying to save the boy, but he fights his way back to *them*. Why would he do that?"

Sheriff Naylor shrugged. "Probably 'cause he loves them."

"Loves them! They're the people who tortured him. *Tortured* him, Sheriff. How do you explain that?"

The sheriff threw up his hands. "Mr. Rinehart, I don't make my living trying to explain things. No future in that."

The soldier lowered his feet to the floor and tried to lay his head back against the couch, but he had a crick in his neck and it wouldn't bend back that far. His knees and elbows and hands hurt. His balls throbbed. He felt sick.

"You know," he said sadly, "for a moment out there I thought of that boy as my own son. The son I might have had, maybe, in another life."

"No sir," Sheriff Naylor said. "No other life. You don't get but one."

The sheriff went on to talk about what was likely to happen to Eddie, who was on his way back to Warsaw now in the deputy's car. But the soldier wasn't listening. He didn't much care.

He interrupted the sheriff in mid-sentence: "Did you know I was born here?"

The soldier didn't know why he'd said it. He hadn't planned to—it was more like he was thinking aloud. But, even though he was so tired he could hardly move, he went on: "Yes, born right here in Jerico. Lived here for seventeen years before I volunteered for the army. But then I guess you'd already figured out I was from here originally."

The sheriff looked at him wonderingly, shook his head.

"No sir," he said. "I wouldn't have figured you to be from anywhere."

The sheriff opened the front door, then turned back once more to the soldier and gave him a long look.

Then he said, "You know, you ought to get out more. Get out amongst the people once in awhile."

The soldier nodded. Then the sheriff was gone. The sound of his car faded toward Warsaw.

The soldier started to get up, but the effort was too much. His breath came in rapid jerks. He felt as if he might faint. But no, he wasn't fainting. The old soldier was sinking dizzily into the vast realization of all that he did not know.

THEM BONES

A LIGHT BREEZE CAME UP JUST as they were ready to start to work and pushed back the low fog that had not yet been scorched off by the July sun, and as the mist receded, Earl Ridgeway could see the figures materialize, wraithlike, among the pines and elms and hickory trees across the road.

He was not surprised. He had expected them. Still, he shivered as they seemed to loom forward out of the trees, although he knew it was the mist retreating from wind and sun and not the figures that moved.

A man has to work. A man has to live.

The foreman was nervous, too, Earl could tell. He'd study the chart, glance across the road and back down at the chart again, scratch his head and shift from one foot to another like he'd lost his place.

Then, with almost miraculous suddenness, the fog lifted, was gone. You would wonder it had been there at all the way the sun sliced down hot and gleaming through the trees.

Earl could see them clearly now except for the ones standing back in the deeper shadows. He could name them off: relative, neighbor, and friend.

The foreman scratched his head, nodded across the road.

"Ridgeway, you're from around here. What do you think those folks are here for?"

"I expect," Earl said, "they're here to watch us raise their dead."

They were mostly college boys on the work crew, one from Sedalia, a couple from Clinton, one or two from Warsaw, a couple from as far away as Kansas City. The rest, another half-a-dozen, were from Jerico, although as it happened most of the Jerico boys were on the other crew, the one working on the new cemetery site up on the hill at the west end of Sunday's Hollow.

Earl was the oldest, twenty-six, and the only one from the Hollow itself on either crew. The boys who had come down from Kansas City and Clinton and Sedalia and Warsaw didn't give a hang what they were doing, of course, and although Jerico was only three or four miles up the road, the people there were naturally all for the dam project. The Harry S Truman dam figured to benefit Jerico immensely, although some snorted that it would only turn the town into one big plywood and neon souvenir stand, just like Eldon and Osage Beach.

Earl looked across the road, then down at his boots.

A man has to work somewhere.

The foreman came back from the pickup, where he

had been talking on the CB.

"Just talked to the big boss," he said, wiping his forehead and sighing. "Seems some preacher or other, Green I think it was, is supposed to say a few words over these folks as we haul 'em up out of the ground. Some deal or other the boss worked out with the preacher to avoid a big hullabaloo. Well—OK, you guys get the tools and that pulley contraption over to that far end over there—might as well start in the shade. Don't start digging, though, until I get the preacher fellow over here."

The workers moved uncertainly into the narrow spaces between the graves, careful not to step on the mounds, although on the far side, where the older graves were, it was not always easy to tell where the mounds had been. Seeing them with their tools and the still unassembled coffin pulley that the company had rented from Laughlin's Funeral Home in Warsaw, the people who had been standing among the trees across the road came forward.

A short, elderly man in a dark blue suit stepped out from the crowd. The Reverend Greene. He bent over his cane, searched the faces of the workers, then let his gaze rest on Earl. Earl looked away.

When the dam was finished, and the water backed up through the hickory and ash and walnut valleys east of Jerico, there wouldn't be a Sunday's Hollow anymore. Earl knew that. Still, when he'd hired on with the big outfit out of Warsaw earlier in the spring, no one had given him any grief about it. A man has to work, and Earl's car insurance had shot up since he had gotten the two speeding tickets and the DWI inside of six months. He had worked on many different jobs for the company since hiring on—clearing woods, building access roads, driving a truck—and seemed to hit all around the Hollow, but as luck would have it he had never had to work in the Hollow itself, which suited him just fine. But dead in the middle of July, he'd been put on a different crew, and Earl knew that there might be trouble.

When the foreman had first told him that they were going to move the graveyard in Sunday's Hollow, Earl had thought with a start of where his grandparents and a dozen aunts and uncles were laid. But the Ridgeways buried in the little cemetery out behind the Calvary Baptist Church, up on a hill on the north side of the Hollow. The water wouldn't reach up there. It was New Hope Baptist that lay at the very bottom of the Hollow, where the generally twisting blacktop stretched out straight for a few hundred yards under the canopied trees. The waters would surely claim it.

Earl was glad he hadn't been on the work crew responsible for tearing down the church building itself. It had been located a hundred yards up the road from the cemetery. One bright, soft April morning Earl had driven past it on his way to a work-site up near Jerico, and when he returned that afternoon, New Hope was gone. They had come in with bulldozers and smashed it, flattened it, hauled off the stones of the foundation and whatever else was salvageable and burned the rest.

Earl had expected some trouble over that, but there was surprisingly little complaining. The people seemed resigned to the inevitable, and, after all, it was just a building. Wood and stone.

The cemetery was another matter. The graves went deep, deep.

When Earl looked back up, the Reverend Greene was no longer staring at him. In fact, Reverend Greene and the foreman were off to the side now, talking, or at least the Reverend was talking and the foreman was listening hard and nodding like he was awfully happy to be agreeing with everything and wanted to make sure the Reverend understood that fact. The people from the Hollow were moving among the graves, contemplating the inscriptions. They didn't look sad so much as interested. They reminded Earl more of tourists than mourners.

But then Earl noticed Floyd Calvin, who had a farm not a quarter-mile away, edging over toward him. Floyd glanced nervously around in that hangdog way of his and pulled his hair back from his forehead with his rough, sun-baked hands.

"It ain't right, Earl."

Earl pushed at the ground with the toe of his boot.

"Ain't right, Earl," Floyd repeated softly but vehemently. "There just ain't nothing right about it. . . . You know that, Earl."

"I know it, Floyd."

"You know that."

"I know it, Floyd, I know it. It's a job is all. You can understand that."

"You sure must be hard up for work, Earl," came a voice from behind him.

Earl turned. It was Francis Oates. Francis wasn't well-liked around the Hollow. He was a little too sharp where money was involved, and he had a violent streak, a mean streak. A drunk, an old bum, had insulted his wife once outside the movie theater in Clinton, and Francis had dragged him into the alley and beat him until he fell to the ground, then made him get up on his knees and apologize to his wife. Then he pulled the drunk's arm up behind his back until it snapped. Jerome Pimm had been in Clinton that night and reported afterward that you could hear the bone crack halfway across the square. Francis was at his worst when he was being self-righteous, which he was most of the time.

"You don't think I'd do this for any other reason, do you?" Earl said.

"Now that I can't answer, Earl. Folks around here can't seem to figure out why you do *anything*."

Earl glared at him a minute, then turned his back and started toward the pickup, where a couple of boys were squatted down in the shade.

As he was walking off, he heard Francis say to Floyd Calvin, much louder than was necessary, "Hell of a great job, ain't it Floyd? . . . Think I'd have more pride."

2.

Folks around Sunday's Hollow never did know what to think of Earl Ridgeway, when they thought of him at all. Earl didn't much know what to think, either.

It was the Vietnam war that had really fouled things up for Earl. He'd gotten a bad number in the lottery in 1971 and had received his draft notice in July. On the day he was supposed to report to the bus depot in Clinton for the ride up to the induction station in Kansas City, he'd gotten up bright and early, stuffed some clothes in a duffle bag, counted his money—fifty-four dollars that he'd managed to save from odd jobs and a twenty-dollar bill that he'd taken from his mother's purse—and hitch-hiked to St. Louis where he got a job working for a painting sub-contractor. The skinflint paid him less that half union wages but paid him in cash, "off the books," no questions asked. He stayed in St. Louis six years.

Two or three times in the first year after Earl took off, some official-looking person would come into the Hollow and ask questions about him. But the Hollow was out-of-the-way from everywhere, and then the war began to wind down, then stopped. Later, talk of amnesty for draft resisters grew. When Earl returned home in 1977, it never occurred to anyone, apparently, that he was a law-breaker, and whatever consequences he should, technically at least, have faced were never brought up by anyone official or unofficial. He had gone, and he was back, and that was that.

Or at least it seemed to be. In fact, Earl was a puzzle. When he first returned from St. Louis, some fellow or other would ask him where his girl was, where the sweet thing from Jefferson City was, and Earl would stare back uncomprehendingly. It was his father who had begun spreading the story after word had gotten out that Earl had failed to show up at the bus station in Clinton.

"Aw, he just took off with this sweet young thing from up by Jeff City," his father would say. "Boy ain't got no sense. Just couldn't be away from his gal. Hot, you know. He'll turn up one of these days."

But when he came back without his girl, and it became evident that there had never been a girl, people began to wonder just why Earl had left. They weren't much worried that he had violated the law. It was a Washington law, after all, in some ways more distant from the people of Sunday's Hollow than the war itself. They knew pain and death.

It hadn't occurred to anyone that Earl might have been a coward. And he wasn't. He couldn't get his mind on the war enough to be afraid of it. That was the big problem.

If he'd had to give a reason for failing to meet that bus in Clinton, Earl would have said it was because he couldn't seem to fix the whole idea of the war in his mind, couldn't see it, couldn't see himself in it. Climbing on that bus represented a two-year commitment to a reality in whose existence he could not bring himself to believe. He had a hard enough time believing in his own reality.

"Why are you here, Earl?" Lacy Sanders had said to Earl about a year ago, right out of the blue, as the two of them and a half-dozen other men were loafing around the Skelley station in Jerico.

It had obviously just popped out because the second he said it Lacy looked around as surprised as anyone else. The others looked at Lacy, puzzled, then looked at Earl, and you could tell by the way they looked at Earl, their surprise softening into contemplation, that they had decided it wasn't a bad question at all. And even though Earl tried to laugh it off, it seemed a pretty good question to him, too.

For a while after Earl returned from St. Louis, people figured he was living at home to help his mother, to help support her and Mr. Ridgeway after Mr. Ridgeway had his stroke. But one day Opal Workman was sympathizing with Earl's mother over Earl getting laid off at the MFA elevator in Jerico, and Mrs. Ridgeway said it didn't really make much difference because Earl would blow his paycheck on his car anyway. Now she'd just have two helpless men around the house instead of one.

There was more than one man around Sunday's Hollow who lived off a woman—mother, wife, lover—and if people didn't exactly approve of it, they didn't pay it much mind. But when you added that to Earl's ducking the draft, plus other things, little things that people couldn't quite put their finger on, well, the fact was that Earl Ridgeway made people uncomfortable, almost as uncomfortable as he made himself.

"One day," old George Workman said when the subject of Earl came up, "Earl Ridgeway is going to blow away in a light breeze. And nobody'll ever remember that he was here."

3.

It was nearly noon, and it was hot. Damn hot.

By ten o'clock the sun had risen over the trees to the east and had begun beating directly down on them. Even the younger boys on the crew had begun to get that pained, dazed look that comes from being caught out under the July sun.

"If you feel you need a blow, go sit over in the shade awhile," the foreman told them. "I don't want nobody burning up on me."

It'd taken them over an hour to finish the first grave. It was the last one on the far east row, one of the old ones, the mound collapsed into the ground. There was no tombstone. Instead, a little rectangular metal marker was stuck into the ground at the head of the grave. The marker was no more than a frame with a glass face into which was inserted a card bearing the name and dates of the deceased. The elements had washed out the ink so that it was impossible to read the name, and the foreman and Reverend Greene pored over the chart—constructed by the Reverend himself from old church records—until the Reverend raised his head and, as if he were announcing the winner of a contest whose prize was of dubious value, meekly called out a name: "Chester Ladurie." The people of the Hollow looked at one another and shrugged. No one could remember a Chester Ladurie, or any other Ladurie for that matter.

The absence of mourners for Chester Ladurie did not stop Reverend Greene from doing things up right. He said a long prayer about the fickleness of man's works, then led the people in singing the first and last verses of "The Old Rugged Cross." Then he nodded to the foreman, and the foreman nodded to the men, and the men began to dig.

It would've been easier if they'd been able to use a backhoe like the foreman wanted, but Reverend Greene would not allow a piece of machinery to be driven over the graves.

"We'll have to use our backbones, boys," the foreman had said.

Earl felt the eyes of the Hollow folk on him as the workers—two or three at a time, there not being room for more—dug solemnly, tentatively, touching the points of their spades against the edges of the grave and pressing delicately, as if they were afraid of making too much noise. When they finally got down near the bottom, they discovered that the coffin was a wooden one, rotted away by moisture and smashed by the weight of the earth so that they brought it up one shattered plank at a time. This was not unforeseen. They had brought along old metal footlockers that the company had purchased from an army surplus store, and as they cleared away the dirt from around the remains of the coffin, two of the boys held up a blanket between the grave and the onlookers, and the planks of the coffin and the bones were placed in the footlockers. It took two of them to hold the planks, bones, and the metal grave marker, which the foreman threw in even though the name on it was no longer legible. After they closed the footlockers, the foreman placed a strip of masking tape on each and wrote the name "Chester Ladurie." The records at his disposal gave no dates for Chester.

His name and his bones.

As they brought the footlockers up out of the grave, Reverend Greene said a prayer whose theme had something to do with eternity, then led the people through four verses of "Rock of Ages."

Reverend Greene said another prayer after they loaded the footlockers into the back of the pickup, and although no one could claim to have known Chester Ladurie, several women began to weep and old Branson Maxwell collapsed against his son and had to be helped into the shade.

"Let's get this goddamn thing out of here," the

foreman hissed, although he had planned to wait and send the coffins up to the new burial site two at a time.

The second grave, which held the remains of Sally Powell, took almost as long as the first. There was a metal coffin, intact, in this one, and it took the boys a while to figure out how to work the pulley. Just as they were about to get the hang of it, Sally's granddaughter, Doris Oates, had tried to throw herself screaming into the open grave, which shook the workers up but didn't surprise anybody else much because Doris liked to do that sort of thing.

After the Dolly Powell grave, though, things began to move faster. The workers began to get into a manageable rhythm, three digging on a grave, two working on the headstone—a job in itself—one driving the pickup and one spelling himself in the shade. Also, the novelty of the thing began to wear off pretty fast for the onlookers. The two or three dozen who had been there when the workers first arrived began to dwindle until by midmorning there were only a handful. The people of the Hollow gradually adjusted themselves to the workers' schedule, and a family would show up only when one of their relatives was about to be brought up from the ground. At the same time, Reverend Greene's enthusiasm for the affair seemed to recede as the sun rose higher. He dropped the hymns entirely after Dolly Powell's grave, and by noon was spending most of his time sitting in a lawn chair in the shade next to George Workman, trading gossip and sipping iced tea from a thermos, hobbling across the road to say an increasingly perfunctory prayer over each new grave. Deacon Pryor was up at the new site saying a few words at each re-interment anyway, he explained, so there wasn't much use in overdoing things.

By noon, for Earl and the rest it was just a job, hot and tiresome, relieved only by telling obscene jokes, goosing each other with the butts of their spades, dreaming of the night.

And then the first stone fell among them.

4.

Instinctively, they looked up at the sky.

Then they looked back down at the stone, which had ricocheted off of Miller ("Chesty") McKewan's tombstone and come to rest at the feet of Darrel Rice, a kid from Kansas City who visited his grandparents in Warsaw every summer and probably lied about his age to get the job with the construction company—he couldn't have been a day over sixteen. Darrel looked down at the stone, which was about the size of a hen's egg.

"Bingo! Look at this."

When he held up the stone between thumb and forefinger, they could see it had a piece of paper wrapped around it, held on with rubber bands.

Darrel stripped the rubber bands off, unwrapped the paper from the stone, which he tossed into a nearby grave.

"Got writing on it. Now let's see, this here says— What in the? . . . What've we got here, a nut or something?"

He frowned at the note, read it to himself again, then let out a loud laugh.

"Haw! Listen to this. 'Do not dig past this row. Leave these bones be. Or you be dead.' Haw!"

They all had to take a look at the note, and after each one read it he'd laugh loudly and pass it on to the next. The foreman came over and took a look and scratched his head, but he didn't laugh.

They looked around. George Workman and Reverend Greene were across the road in the shade, chewing the fat, paying them no attention. Several members of the Burns family, no doubt waiting for them to get to Clovis Burns, sat inside their cars, the doors swung open, looking bored and bedraggled in the heat. No one else was to be seen.

"What do you make of this, Earl?" the foreman asked.

"You got me."

The foreman looked down at the note again, then marched across the road. They watched him speak to Reverend Greene, then hand him the note. The Reverend and George Workman read the note, and the three talked for a while. Then the foreman came back to the work crew.

"A joke of some sort, the preacher figures. Says folks around here are law-abiding citizens. That the way you see it, Earl?"

"Well . . ."

They went back to work. Shortly they had Chesty McKewan out of the ground and were ready to dig on Teresa McKewan, Chesty's sister, who had died an old maid. The foreman said after they finished on her, they'd break for lunch.

They'd just begun to dig when Bill Emerson let out

a yell and flung his spade down.

"Bill! What's the matter!"

"Some son-of-a-bitch just got me with a rock, that's what's the matter!"

He gingerly rubbed his arm and scrunched his face up like he was ready to cry.

"Maybe it was just a bee," Darrel Rice said.

Bill reached down and picked up a golf-ball-sized rock and held it next to his left elbow, where a fiery red knot had already swollen up to almost the size of the stone.

The boys began to get excited and wanted to strike off into the woods in search of whoever was out there. No, said the foreman. He told them to go back to work but appointed Bill Emerson, who still looked much aggrieved over his elbow, to act like he was working on Teresa McKewan's tombstone. Instead of working, though, he was to keep his eye on the woods and let out a holler if he saw anyone.

They hadn't been at it five minutes when a rock whistled past Earl's ear, and at almost the same instant Bill Emerson let out a whoop.

"There he is, boys! Get 'im!"

They all took off toward the woods in the direction Bill had pointed, the foreman following close behind and hollering for them to come back, come back, come back! They ignored him and hit the line of trees like a football team hitting a line of defenders on a kickoff.

But once into the woods they became caught up in the surprisingly thick underbrush—like a damn jungle, Earl heard one of them say. Earl was more used to the woods and picked his way through easily and surely while the others thrashed and cursed at the brambles and tree limbs. The woods began to clear somewhat where a hill rose up out of the valley toward their left, and the others veered off into this more open space and moved away from Earl.

Earl knew that whoever it was they were after was unlikely to move into an area where he could more easily be seen, so he stayed in the denser woods and worked his way toward the creek.

After about a hundred yards the clotted foliage became somewhat less thick as the ground sloped away toward the bank of the Grand North. He walked along the bank and gazed down at the creek—now starved to a dusty trickle by the summer sun. A few yards ahead, a run-off from the hill had eroded a cut about two yards wide into the bank down to the bed of the creek. The opening to the cut was covered with brush. Earl walked up to it and peered down.

"Come on in, Earl," a soft voice invited.

Earl looked over his shoulder to make sure none of the others had followed, then pushed back the brush and slid down into the cut.

"Howdy, Vernon," he said.

Vernon scooted down the large tree limb that ran the length of the cut, motioned politely for Earl to sit.

"How'd you spot me in here, Earl?"

Earl nodded at Vernon's red shirt.

"Shouldn't wear bright colors if you're going to try something like this, Vernon."

"I reckon that's right," Vernon nodded. "That's something they taught you boys over in Viet Nam, I guess."

Earl let it pass.

Vernon Sessions. He hadn't really thought of Vernon Sessions. He was a shy little guy, getting on in years now, who lived on a small farm over nearer the east end of the Hollow. His wife had died a few years before, and she must be the one buried on the next row, the row mentioned in the note. They were one of those quiet couples who could live near a person for decades, then pass on and be no more thought of than ashes in the wind.

Earl grinned at Vernon and said, "You still got a pretty good arm on you."

Vernon shook his head and smiled, a little sadly.

"Not much of one. I chucked a half-dozen rocks over there before I finally hit anybody. Couldn't even get close enough to get you all to take notice."

"You sure made that one boy yelp," Earl said, laughing.

"Well, Earl, I was aiming at you with all of them."

Earl was taken aback.

"Vernon. I'm surprised at you."

"I'm surprised at you, too, Earl," Vernon said quietly.

"Look, Vernon, it's only a job."

"There's all sorts of ways to make a living, Earl. And all sorts of ways to live."

"Jesus H., Vernon. What's everybody jumping me about? First Floyd, then Francis, now you. There's a lot of guys working around here. How come I'm the one seems to be carrying that dam on my back?"

"Maybe folks figure you should know better, Earl, being from around here."

"I don't see what me being from around here has

got to do with anything."

"No, I don't guess you would."

Earl shook his head. What did people want of him? He felt like grabbing the little old son-of-a-bitch and wringing his neck.

Instead, he shrugged and said, "Vernon, have you seen that new cemetery up on top of the hill? Where we're moving the graves? Real pretty up there, Vernon. Birds'll be singing . . ."

"Birds sing down here."

"Wind'll be blowing nice . . ."

"She didn't like the wind. She was cold a lot as she got older."

"She'll rest easy up there, Vernon."

Vernon looked away.

"No," he said softly, "she won't."

"Why not?"

"Cause I promised her, 'Sweetheart,' I said, 'We'll lie side by side in the valley.'"

Earl tried to remember Sally. Tiny woman, frail, gingham dress. Or was that someone on "Little House on the Prairie"? A tiny woman, frail . . . No, he couldn't remember.

"Vernon, you can lie side by side forever, up on the hill."

"The valley," he said. "I promised her the valley."

"Vernon, I just don't understand."

Vernon turned back to Earl and smiled at him sadly but almost kindly. "You don't understand nothing, Earl."

Vernon stared at Earl musingly for several moments.

"Had a dog once, when I was a boy," he said finally. "Loved that dog. Just a mutt. He got kicked in the neck by a horse and choked to death. I didn't see it. My daddy came home from the fields and told me about it. I cried so hard I tore some stomach muscles. They had to take me all the way in to Clinton to a doctor. A real trip back then, and my daddy couldn't really spare the money—but he took me."

He stopped. Earl waited for him to continue, but he didn't say any more. I don't understand, Earl started to say, but then he let it go. It was well past time for lunch, and he was tired of stories and explanations and trying to figure things out. People made everything too damn complicated.

"Well, Vernon," he sighed, "what do you want me to do?"

"You've got to figure that out for yourself, Earl."

"Quit? You expect me to up and quit?"

"That'd be right neighborly."

Earl started to laugh but stopped when he saw that Vernon wasn't joking.

"Hell now. If I quit they'll just bring in somebody else to do the job."

"Probably so. You can't always help what winds up being done, but you can do your damnedest not to be part of it."

"You're living in a dream world, Vernon."

Vernon shook his head and looked away again. Earl followed his gaze down into the bottom of the cut, where it met the creek bed. All that he could see of it now was bone dry. In the spring, though, water would come swelling brown and rich halfway up the bank, and after a long, heavy rain the water would rush down between the hills and burst out across the fields west of Jerico.

"You do what you got to do, Earl," Vernon said in his weary, sad, and resolute voice, "and I'll do what I got to do."

*

Earl made his way out of the woods and back to the pickup. The others, hot and hungry and tired of the chase, showed up in a few minutes, and they all climbed into the pickup and rode back into Warsaw for lunch. Earl said nothing about seeing Vernon Sessions.

When they got back from lunch, they found a canning jar on the first grave of the second row. There was a note inside: DO NOT DIG ON THIS ROW. LET THESE BONES BE.

Or you be dead.

5.

"We got it pretty much narrowed down to two people who might've done it," Eugene Naylor said, unconsciously fiddling with his sheriff's badge as he talked. "We figure it's got to be either Vernon Sessions or Junior Schneider."

Sheriff Naylor paused, evidently waiting for Earl to react. Earl said nothing, closed his eyes against a wave of nausea.

Sheriff Naylor went on.

"We figure it's somebody on the second row he don't want dug up—that's plain from the notes. Most of the folks still around here who've got kin buried on the second row have pretty much been accounted for, except for Vernon and Junior. Junior might be on a toot up in Sedalia or someplace. It's hard to see him getting sober enough to pull off a stunt like this anyway. Vernon, now, he's harder to figure. You think it could have been Vernon Sessions, Earl?"

Earl said nothing. Time after time today he'd been told about what he didn't understand, what he didn't know, so he saw no reason to open his mouth now. Besides, the painkiller not only was making him vaguely nauseous but also drowsy. All he wanted to do was sleep. He hadn't actually seen Vernon, of course. No one had. They'd returned from their lunch break, found the jar and note, tossed them away. They'd posted a guard, filled their pockets with rocks in case of another attack, and set to work on the second row. Sally Sessions' grave was almost in the middle of the row, fourth from the end. Earl could think of nothing else at first, but the sun was so high and hot, with no shade, and the digging so hard that after the second grave he could think of nothing but the breathless heat.

And then he found himself on the ground, staring into the sun, the trees on the periphery of his vision spinning and tilting crazily. *Heat stroke!* he'd thought. And it wasn't until he saw the sun and the dancing trees and thought *Heat stroke!* that he finally heard the sound of the blast crashing off through the Hollow. Even then it didn't

occur to him that he'd been shot until he rolled to his left, saw the other workers diving behind tombstones and grave mounds, two even vaulting into an open grave, and felt the shocking pain blaze through his shoulder.
And then he blacked out.

When he came to, he was in the Benton County Community Health Center, a long, low, one-storey brick building where his father had lain for over three months trying to survive his stroke.

The small caliber bullet had somehow missed bone and major arteries and come out just to the side of his shoulder blade, but it had torn up some muscle. When he came to, they already had him patched up, his arm taped tight to his side, forearm in a sling.

The doctor told him they'd admit him for the night, or he could go home when his mother got there, whichever he felt like. Earl said he'd just as soon go on home.

He thanked the doctor for his time and the bottle of pain killers and promised to be there the next morning to be checked over again. He didn't say any more to Sheriff Naylor, who didn't press the issue.

Earl would not turn Vernon in for shooting him; he knew that, although he didn't quite know why he wouldn't. And he didn't know why he had the sense that things were not over for him and Vernon, even now, that there was still something left for them to do.

*

After bringing Earl home, his mother had gone back to work—she hated to miss work; she needed the money—and he had dozed, then got up and walked around the house, holding on to chairs, tables, the wall with his good hand to support himself. He vomited into the daisy bed off the side of the porch, took two more pain pills, dozed, got up and roamed the house again, and had been standing in front of his father for about five minutes when his mother returned from work.

He had wanted to say something to his father, but he didn't know what it was. It had seemed important.

His father had sat there staring up at him with the biding patience of the invalid. His right hand trembled on the arm of the wheelchair, the right side of his face perpetually twisted into a melancholy sneer. His father could walk, or at least could shuffle along fairly well using a crutch and dragging his right foot, setting it down with a triumphant *thud* at each step, but he would forget where he was going, and if he was outside and turned his back on the house, he would forget where the house was and grow frightened. With an effort he could make himself understood, but he would sound as if he were trying to talk around a stone in his mouth. Mostly, he sat in his wheelchair and did nothing at all.

Earl's mother came up behind him and laid a hand on his good shoulder, looking hesitantly from Earl to his father, his father to Earl.

Earl wanted to say something.

Finally, his mother said, "Daddy, Earl's been shot."

His father shifted around in his wheelchair, frowned.

"Earl's been shot, Daddy."

Suddenly, his father stopped fidgeting, and his face smoothed out in a look of bright wonder.

"Pup 'art!" he croaked.

Earl and his mother exchanged puzzled looks.

In the effort to speak clearly, the sad sneer broadened into a smile.

"Pu'ple Heart!" he finally managed to say, then he relaxed, beaming proudly at his son.

*

Shortly after nightfall Sheriff Naylor came over to tell them that, sure enough, Junior Schneider had turned up drunk as a one-eyed Chinaman in Sedalia, had been there all day, apparently. They hadn't found Vernon Sessions yet but were still looking for him. Earl shouldn't worry, they'd find him.

At around nine that night Earl took a pain pill, then an hour later couldn't remember when he'd last taken one and took another. He went to bed, his ears buzzing, feeling tired and weak as a jar of warm jelly.

But he couldn't sleep. Images from the day flitted through his head so fast that no sooner would he almost have one in focus then it was gone and another there, then gone, then another. He grew dizzy, rolled in sweat and wept when he recalled the dog that he'd had when he was a little boy, the one that'd gotten kicked in the head and killed and he'd buried in the back yard and then dug up and taken with him in his suitcase to St. Louis, but he couldn't remember the dog's name because there'd never been a dog and he wept for the dog he'd never had.

It must have been after midnight when he took his father's crutch and started off down the road toward the cemetery. He would steal a march . . .

He shouldn't have been able to make it from the front porch to the blacktop, but somehow he made it there and on up the first hill, using the crutch like a one-armed ferryman poling his way upstream. But on the down-slope the crutch caught in a pothole, and he fell and rolled most of the way to the bottom—a good way to make time, he thought, and almost laughed except somebody was jabbing a bayonet into his shoulder again and again. He got up and walked on, weeping and hurting and weary unto death, and it might have taken him two hours to get there or two years or two minutes or no time or all time because time didn't count anymore but only the pain, which wasn't fair because it wouldn't stay in his shoulder where the hole was but burst through his whole body with each step. Weeping. And weariness unto death.

He got there.

He stumbled into the second row of graves and noticed that Sally Sessions' grave had been dug on. It was a black rectangle on the night shadows, and he couldn't tell how far down they'd gotten, whether they'd gotten her up or not. He didn't think about it much. He didn't have much time, and he had to get something said.

"Vernon!" he shouted, or tried to shout. He wasn't sure the name had come out at all, he was so weak. He suddenly thought of his father, trying to talk around the big stone in his mouth. But he didn't have time to think of that, either. He had to get it said, something said, he wasn't sure what until he said it.

"Vernon, I'm not digging up any more graves, I just come to tell you that. I don't know what it means, I don't know what good it'll do, but I'm through digging up graves. OK, Vernon?"

The trees around him were dark and silent.

"I didn't know it'd bother people so much, but I guess it does, so I'm through with it. I wish I could tell you it'll change things. I wish you and Sally could stay here forever, Vernon, but one man can't make that happen. At least, I don't see how . . . I don't see . . ."

He sat down on the ground by Sally's grave. He could see now that they'd gotten no more than a couple of feet down. But they'd be back. Dig her up. What he did, what a man did . . . He wished he could see . . .

He wished for a sign. In the Bible . . . it wasn't fair. In the Bible . . . there'd be a sign. Pillar of fire. Go this way. Stay here. Do this, and this will follow. Count on it. Promised land.

He lay down next to Sally.

Promised land. Purple Heart. Sweetheart. Pillar of fire.

6.

His mother found him on the front porch next morning and was helping him to his feet when she suddenly stopped and looked over her shoulder at the column of smoke that stood up straight and solemn in the bright sky.

"What on earth—?"

Earl thought she was referring to his being out on the porch, and he searched for an explanation, but none came to him because he couldn't remember how he got there. The last thing he remembered was lying down by Sally Sessions' grave. When the sun woke him, he was stretched out on the front porch.

Then Earl noticed that his mother wasn't looking at him. He turned and saw the smoke. It was hard to judge its distance. It could have been in the next field just beyond the trees, or miles away.

"Let's go," he said, pulling away from his mother, at the same time losing his balance, and grabbing back onto her for support.

"Go where?"

"Down to the cemetery."

"You're crazy, Earl. You'd fall over if a feather hit you. Come on into the house."

"Forget it, then," he said. "I'll walk it."

He released her and took two or three wobbly steps toward the edge of the porch.

"Earl!"

*

"You got to admire the old boy," Sheriff Naylor said, shielding his eyes from the smoke. "He did a hell of a night's work."

In the time it'd taken Earl's mother to make sure that his father was taken care of, then help Earl into the car, then drive the two miles to the cemetery, a breeze had come up and was blowing the smoke first one way then the other, and the onlookers shifted restlessly around to keep clear of it.

"You boys hadn't even started on Sally's grave yesterday when work was called off, yet old Vernon managed to dig that grave all by hisself, then somehow, by hisself, rig that pulley and get the casket up out of the grave."

Yes, and carry me home, Earl suddenly realized. Or did he have a car? How did he manage it? Could a man do so much? It didn't seem reasonable to think it.

"Course, her casket wasn't metal, I guess, and didn't weigh so awful much She was wood; that's why she's burning so good."

Earl staggered up close to the pyre, but the heat drove him back. He shielded his eyes against the stinging heat and stared hard, but the smoke from the branches and small logs—too green, probably—was so dense that he couldn't see anything.

"Vernon Sessions!" he screamed.

"Yep. It was Vernon, all right. Dug her up, hauled up that casket, gathered up all that wood—all on his own. Now what do you figure was the point of that?"

"Vernon Sessions!"

Earl staggered in toward the pyre, but the flames drove him back again. He peered into the fire, but he couldn't see. He took a step forward, hesitated, then retreated.

"Vernon Sessions!"

MEMORIAL DAY

AFTER THE FIRST SHOCK OF THE COLD water, George begins to relax, and then as the water slowly warms, his eyes close, and his chin falls down onto his hairless chest, blue-veined like fine marble. Slumping back against the wall of the shower, he looks as if he might be asleep. It is always this way. Gently, she pulls him forward away from the wall and turns him this way and that so the water can wash over his back, sides, under his arms, over his legs, privates, feet. He is so tall that, even stooped as he is in his old age, she has to stretch up on tiptoe to ladle water from her cupped hands over his wispy grey hair. Even stooped as he is, George is taller than Johnny, she thinks.

Stretching up, she scrubs shampoo into his hair, then rinses it off with handfuls of water. She lathers up soap between her palms, washes his face and neck, digs her fingers into the folds and creases of his ears. She rinses his face off immediately so that his skin, which looks thin and brittle as a page torn from an old Bible, will not chap and crack. Then she washes his chest, arms, and back. As she soaps and rinses, she kneads his flesh and the remnant of muscle that rolls like loose cords over his bones. George likes this. He almost smiles and makes a sound in the back of his throat like a cat purring.

When she soaps between his legs, sometimes his penis doesn't stiffen so much as stretches out, hangs limply down past the shrunken bald bag of his scrotum, as if in the fog of his mind George is half-remembering some thing that stirred his young blood once. When this happens, she always grows sad, not for what George remembers but for what he has forgotten, for all that bone, blood and seed forgets as it stumbles its way toward death.

Always, toward the end of the shower George will grow cold again, no matter how warm she keeps the water, and he will begin to tremble. It is then that she takes him in her arms and presses him to her warm, plump body. She rubs his flesh, hugs him tight, tight, and coos some almost tuneless lullaby into his smooth chest. She holds him until his breathing calms and his trembling stops, holds him for a few moments more after she turns off the water.

George likes this.

Sometimes, when the water is off and he is warm in her embrace, George stares down at her, and a soft looks comes into his eyes. It may be love.

"Opal," he says.

"No," she says sadly, "I'm Maureen."

*

"Maureen?" came the voice, suddenly there, almost on top of her.

Maureen jumped like she'd been shot. She'd been scrubbing away at the shower stall with the stiff-bristled brush, and she hadn't heard the car pull into the drive, the door open and close.

She scrambled to her feet and peeked around the door of the stall. It was Ella, George's sister, come down from Sedalia. They didn't stand on ceremony in the Workman family—no engraved invitations for them. That was fine with Maureen—she was just people too—but the state Ella'd caught her in!

"Oh my, it looks like I've come at a bad time," Ella said.

"Oh no, that's OK, Ella. I just got through getting George cleaned up and dressed, and I was trying to get things straightened out here. I'm afraid I'm a real mess."

"Now don't you think a thing about it, Maureen. Somebody drops in out of the blue, they're not a guest, they're a nuisance. I'll let myself in and go talk to George. You just go on about your business."

"It'll take me just a few minutes to get cleaned up, then I'll make us a pot of coffee."

"Now, you just go on about your business, Maureen," Ella repeated, disappearing into the house.

Even after Ella was gone, Maureen felt herself blushing. Caught like that, wearing one of Johnny's old raggedy terrycloth robes and not a stitch else, down on her hands and knees, her bare feet and big behind sticking out the door!

She liked Ella, who was almost as old as George and bent and gnarled by arthritis, but still alert and spry, an independent woman who drove her own car, kept up her own house and still mowed the lawn herself. She liked Ella but was afraid Ella didn't like her—or didn't approve of her at least. It probably wasn't in Ella to actually dislike anyone, but she was a strict Baptist like all the Workmans, except Johnny, and Maureen felt sure she disapproved of her and Johnny living together without the benefit of marriage. The truth was it bothered Maureen too. But although Johnny had told he loved her, over and over in their first couple of years together, he'd never asked her to marry him. What could she do? She was in her mid-forties, after all—too darned old to cry about it.

Maureen went back to scrubbing the inside of the shower stall. But "shower stall" was too fancy a term for what was more a shed or tall box jerryrigged to the side of the house next to the kitchen door. Johnny had built it for himself to use when he came in hot and dusty from work in the fields, but Maureen had taken it over now. Not that it was really her choice. She'd rather use the bathtub—wouldn't have to worry about George falling—but Johnny had spoiled that when he came in drunk one day determined to use the bathtub to clean off an old crankshaft from a tractor he was overhauling. Maureen warned him the cleaning solution might ruin the enamel on the tub, but he hadn't even gotten that far, stumbling and dropping the crankshaft, which knocked a hole in the tub big enough to lose your foot in. Johnny promised he'd fix the tub, but then Johnny made a lot of promises.

She scrubbed at the stall.

Now Johnny wouldn't use the shower any more, instead taking sponge baths at the kitchen sink. He said he wasn't going to take a shower in a stall that old man used as a urinal. It was true George often lost control of his bladder when he relaxed in the warm water. That's why Maureen spent half her life down on her hands and knees scrubbing. But it didn't make any difference to Johnny—he still refused to use it.

Johnny had built it out of clapboard planks he'd ripped off the back of the old Workman place—the house Johnny had grown up in, George's house and George's parents' before him—down the hill not two hundred yards away. If it weren't for the stand of hickory and pine and elm trees on the other side of the cornfield, it would be easy to see the Workman place right there from Johnny and Maureen's house. Johnny's house, call it. Was it Maureen's? What did she have, anyway, that was hers?

"Why didn't you just rip them off the front while you were at it, Johnny?" Ella had said one day after taking a walk down to the old place. "I know where the wood for that shower came from. You don't fool me or anyone else."

Her words were bitter—she'd grown up there too, after all—and Johnny had stormed out of the house. Now they avoided one another, and Maureen felt caught between them.

Maureen rinsed the Spic 'n Span off the shower walls, dried her feet on the hem of the faded blue robe, and *flopped flopped* back into the house in her rubber thongs.

She intended to put a pot of coffee on, then quick get dressed while it was brewing, but Ella walked into the kitchen before she could get the Norelco plugged in. She was hugging one of George's old leather photo albums to her chest; she looked stricken.

"Why Ella, is something wrong?"

Ella hugged the album tighter.

"They weren't just George's, you know," she said.

She looked ready to cry.

Maureen stared at her uncomprehendingly.

"The pictures—they weren't just George's. They were mine, too."

Ella handed her the album carefully and sorrowfully, as if were a stillborn baby that she'd carried to term, lavished hopes and dreams on. Maureen turned the pages dumbly. Here and there was a picture, mostly of people she didn't know, but on every page were blank spaces bracketed by glued-on photo corners, and on many pages were no photos at all.

"He didn't have any right to take them," Ella said. "They were my folks, too. There were pictures in there when we were all kids—George and Mary and me. I didn't complain when he took things from the house I didn't even complain about the money. But those pictures were memories, Maureen. When you get to be my age, that's about all you've got left."

Maureen didn't know what to say. She made a half-hearted attempt to hand the album back to Ella, but she turned her head and wrinkled up her nose as if something smelled bad. But then she turned back to Maureen.

"Do you know what he did with them, Maureen? If you do, please tell me. He can keep the originals. Just give them to me long enough to have copies made."

"I'm so sorry, Ella, but I just don't know anything about it."

Ella nodded and grimaced as if she'd expected as much. Then she sighed.

"Well, I'm going to go on over to the cemetery. I brought some flowers for Momma and Daddy. I'd take George, but he wouldn't know anything about it anyway."

Maureen was shocked. Ever since George had begun to suffer from Alzheimer's, Ella had been a rock for him. He'd lost ground over the last few months. He seemed aware of hardly anything, spoke rarely, except once in a while out of the blue a few words about "the grove," as he called it, where he and Opal, his wife, used to take picnics—when they were young, Maureen guessed. Opal had been dead for close to twenty years, and Johnny cut the grove down years ago, before Maureen moved in with him, when he was clearing land for the new pasture. Still, it was the only thing George ever spoke a full sentence about any more. Despite that, despite his not being able to feed himself or control his bodily functions, Ella never treated him like a baby or simply ignored him as Johnny did more and more. She'd talk to him just like he understood, take him on drives to get ice cream or to look at the boats on the lake. Until today, that is, until this . . . her bitterness too much for her.

Maureen followed Ella on out to her car. Ella stood by the door of the car a minute as if debating something with herself, then turned to Maureen, smiling like her old self.

"When I get back from the cemetery, I want to take George over to the White Branch Cafe for dinner. George always likes the White Branch."

"That's real nice of you, Ella, but you know George doesn't do too good on his own anymore."

Ella laughed.

"Oh, George and I will do fine. We'll have a gay old time!"

After Ella had driven out of the yard, Maureen went back into the house. Before she even got inside

George's room, she smelled it.

"Oh no, George, not again, not so soon."

Seated in his rocker, the old pink shower curtain wrapped around the cushions to protect them from his "accidents," George stared up at the ceiling, his mouth open.

Maureen leaned down over the rocker, pressed his head against her breast, laid her cheek against his hair, fine as corn silk.

"Not so soon, George, not so soon."

He pulled away and gazed back at her, a puzzled look on his face. Then he smiled that small, warm smile.

"Opal?" he said.

*

She cannot turn the water on first and allow it to warm up, because then George won't go in. He'll stand with his feet spread and lean back, stubborn as a cow that refuses to go through a gate. So she has to guide him in first, then follow him in, take her robe off and hang it from the nail just outside the door, then turn the water on.

She tries to shield him when the water comes out cold, tries to block the water with her body, puts her hands up in front of his face, turns her long thick brown hair—her best feature, she knows, even though the style is too young for her, much too young—into the spray. But she can't protect him completely, and when the water hits him he stiffens, a look of surprise and fear on his face. As the water warms, though, he begins to relax, and she massages the slack flesh and muscle of his neck, shoulders, and arms, and he leans against her and smiles and purrs.

"We'll eat among the lilacs," he says. "We'll lie in the

shade of . . ."
"The maple trees," she offers.
He is speaking of the grove again, his and Opal's grove,
which is no longer there. Maureen wishes she could have seen
the grove. She wishes she could see all that George has forgot-
ten.
She washes, she rinses. She hugs him close.

*

She heard his pickup before she saw it, coming
around the cornfield the back way, up the old rutted road,
really an old cattle trail more than a road, and for the
briefest moment she wondered why he was coming that
way instead of straight up the blacktop, so much faster
and easier. But then of course she realized what it was.
Johnny only came the back way from the Workman place
when he'd taken something that belonged to Ella and
Mary—Ella and George's sister, a widow living over in
Clinton—just as much as it belonged to him, or to his sis-
ter Jackie Lee, who hadn't spoken to him since the blow-
up over the money. At least she guessed they had as
much right to it. Johnny didn't think so. He said he and
Maureen were looking after the old man now, taking care
of him night and day, so they had a right to it. Everything.
Once she would have believed him, whatever he told her,
but that seemed like a long time ago. She didn't know
Johnny now. Maybe she'd never known him.

The pickup was all the way into the yard before
she noticed the white object in the bed, belly up, feet
sticking up in the air like a drowned, bloated sow. A bath-
tub.

Johnny climbed out of the pickup and slammed the door, looked at her and then away, defiant and hangdog at the same time.

"Well, you wanted me to fix the goddamn bathtub, didn't you?"

"Yes."

Maureen was glad Ella was gone with George to Warsaw.

"Ella came by, Johnny. She took George in to eat at the White Branch."

"Pop and Ella at the White Branch. Ha! That'd be a goddamn sight. I'd about pay to see that one."

Johnny leaned into the pickup and gave a little tug on the bathtub, stopped. He ran his arm across his forehead, studied the tub, then turned back to Maureen with a startled look as if for a moment he'd forgotten she was there.

*

Johnny was still standing by the pickup as she drove her old Chevette out of the yard and turned onto the blacktop. He was a big man, broad shouldered, heavy armed, beer belly stretching his T-shirt. Still, it must have been a job horsing that bathtub into the pickup by himself. Maybe Maureen should have stayed to help him get it out, but then he hadn't asked for her help, and for some reason she was anxious to get away.

As she drove off down the blacktop, she thought she heard him call out "Maureen," but maybe she just imagined it. She didn't look back.

Maureen. She'd never liked her name. She didn't

know a single other Maureen, hadn't known one when she was a girl. Even then it had seemed an old-fashioned sort of name, like Mable or Esther or Ida. Worse, when she thought of "Maureen" she thought of some rather hopeless woman, a little too heavy, a little too slow, not very pretty, someone other women would like well enough because "Maureen" would be good-natured and because she'd be no sort of threat, no competition. They'd like her, but not *really* like her, not get close to her. Men, if they thought about her at all, would think about her second or third or fourth, after they'd thought of all the other women who were slimmer, brighter, prettier than "Maureen."

Once when she was thirteen, Maureen had spanned her ankle front to back with thumb and forefinger, then big knobby bone on the left to big knobby bone on the right. Her ankle was *that* big. She had sat bent over with her hand around her ankle and cried, remembering her mother, years before when she was still alive, saying, "You can do something about your weight, and you can do something about your hair, and you can do something about your skin, but you can't never do *nothing* about your ankles." Maureen had never understood why her mother had said that, out of the blue apparently, but bent over, measuring her ankles, suddenly it came to her. And Maureen cried.

If she allowed herself to think about it enough, she could cry right now. But she didn't. There wasn't much use in crying over something like that once you'd reached forty-five.

She drove past the old Workman place. From the blacktop you wouldn't know that Johnny had ripped planks off the back—or that he'd taken all that stuff from inside: furniture, light fixtures, throw rugs, a space heater, now plumbing fixtures. Why did he do it? At first he said it was for George, to make him feel at home in his new house, but Maureen knew that not everything ended up in their house. Some of it he sold. And then there was the pie safe, a valuable antique in almost perfect condition, which he'd dragged outside and broke up with an ax, taking great gulps of beer between swings of the ax, with a look on his face that frightened her. Why was he in such a rage?

The blacktop abruptly ended at a barricade of steel girders, and she turned left and drove up the access road to the new highway. Years ago—before she'd met Johnny— the blacktop had wound down through a little valley they'd called Sunday's Hollow. But that was before the Truman Dam was built. Now one long arm of the lake backed up through the Hollow almost to the doorstep of the Workman place, and to get to Warsaw you had to take the new highway, then cross the long bridge. Maureen had grown up in Warsaw, not the Hollow like Johnny, but still she felt a nostalgia for it, and something else—unease that things wouldn't stay put. Things, places—people— would change right in front of your eyes.

Traffic on the highway was heavy because of the three-day weekend, and by the time she crossed the bridge and got into the edge of Warsaw—a tourist center since the dam went in—it was bumper to bumper.

Slowly, the line of cars crept past the Lakeside Video. It had been the first video store in Warsaw and was where Maureen was working when she met Johnny. She'd seen him around before, though, and knew him by

reputation. People said he was wild and rough, a woman-
izer and a hard drinker, but he didn't seem that way to
her, not at first. He'd looked around the store for a while,
then brought a tape up to the counter. It was "triple-X"
rated—on the cover was a man pressing himself up
behind a nude woman, his hands covering her breasts,
digging in, the flesh swelling around his fingers like
bread dough.

"Look at this," he'd said. "How can you work in a
place that sells filth like this? You're too good for this
trash."

You could have knocked her over with a feather.

Her next night off he drove her up to Lincoln for
smorgasbord at Riddley's, then the following Sunday
took her to church at Calvary Baptist. Soon he was telling
her that she was the woman for him, that he loved her,
wanted her, but didn't want her in the back seat of a car
or in some cheap motel—she was too good for that—but
wanted her to come and live with him. He'd build a new
house for her, he said.

And then—a miracle—he actually did it. Built the
house up on the hill, just him and his buddy Herman Kile
doing all the work. It was no palace, small, with thin walls
that radiated heat in the summer and trembled in the cold
winter winds, but she felt like Cinderella who'd awak-
ened one day to find herself married to the prince. If
Johnny was no prince and they weren't married, it didn't
matter so much. He'd done more for her than any other
man.

Then things began to change. First there was that
terrible scene with Jackie Lee, her screaming and crying,
saying Johnny had stolen everything from George, gotten

him to sell off half his land when he wasn't competent to make that decision, then kept all the money himself, spent it on the new house and the truck. She said she was going to get a lawyer. Johnny said fine, go right ahead, but a lawyer wasn't going to bring her back from the dead, and Maureen remembered the talk about how wild and dangerous Johnny was, and she thought maybe they weren't just tales. Jackie Lee had never come back to the house after that although Maureen ran into her once in a while in Warsaw. "You're a saint, Maureen," Jackie Lee would say, "but that man you're living with is the devil himself."

Maureen pulled into the IGA and bought a half-gallon of ice cream—Tin Roof, she remembered Ella liked that—then turned back for home. The traffic was just as bad going back; the day was getting hot; the air conditioner had gone out on the Chevette two years ago, and Johnny had never gotten around to fixing it, although he'd promised to often enough. On a whim, Maureen turned off the highway into a little picnic area overlooking the lake. She threw her door open to catch the breeze and sat looking at the calm, deep-blue water.

It was strange to think that not so very long ago there down beneath the water had been roads, fields, barns, houses. How utterly everything had changed. How did it happen? Had she changed? She didn't think so. She felt she was the same old Maureen she'd always been, the Maureen who'd been so happy that Johnny had come along and taken her out of that video store, that hopeless life of loneliness and occasional one-night stands with men who probably wouldn't remember her name a week afterward, men who acted like she should be grateful they paid a little attention to this thick-ankled woman. And she *was* grateful—to Johnny for getting her out of that. She would have been satisfied with the badly built little house, not being married, having a failing old man to care for, satisfied with it all if only Johnny hadn't changed.

When did the change come? Was it winning that *Clinton Eye* contest? To celebrate its one-hundredth anniversary the *Eye* invited subscribers to tell them in twenty-five words or less why it was their favorite newspaper. Although she couldn't remember him spending much time with the paper, Johnny had surprised her by filling out the entry form. "I read the *Clinton Eye*," he wrote, "because it keeps an eye on the truth." Everybody but Johnny was stunned when he won.

"Why hell, you didn't expect anything else to top that one, did you?"

He won a one-hundred dollar U. S. savings bond, a ten-year subscription to the *Eye*, and two free dinners at Wiley's Cafe.

Afterward, he began to act like he owned the truth—the very word itself—and no one else had a right to use it. To almost any comment or observation someone made Johnny would say something like "That is the absolute truth" or "That, let me tell you, is nowhere close to the truth." If anyone else dared to comment on something relating to the truth, Johnny would scoff, "Hell, you wouldn't know the truth if it jumped up and bit you on the ass."

"Damn, Johnny, you're getting hard to live with," Damon Pierce, who worked down at the MFA, said to him one day. "Well, you're one lucky son-of-a-bitch, then, ain't you, Damon, since you don't have to live with me,"

Johnny shot back. Even his best friend, Herman Kile, had gotten fed up. "Hell, Johnny, don't you know they just drew the damn thing out of a box?" he said. "You don't think they actually gave a damn what it said on it, do you? Ha! I'm telling you, they just drew it out of a box!" They were sitting in a bar in Warsaw when Herman said it, and Johnny turned and hit him on the cheekbone and knocked him off the barstool. "He's a lucky man I hit him with my left and not my right," Johnny said afterward. "If I'd hit him with my right, he'd be a dead man now. And that's the truth."

He lost all of his friends. He stopped driving the truck, sold it, bought a tractor, sold that. He said he was a farmer now, but except for a little corn and a few head of cattle, Maureen couldn't see that he did much farming. She suspicioned that he lived by selling off parcels of George's land a little at a time, but she wasn't sure. Johnny never talked to her about things like that. He spent a lot of his time anymore down at the Workman place taking one thing after another, selling some of it, but not all, bringing most of it back up to their house. Even though she'd been down to the Workman place a number of times herself—no particular reason, just out for a walk—it wasn't until recently that it occurred to her that Johnny had built his new house on almost exactly the same plan, same dimensions, as the old one. When he brought a piece of furniture or a throw rug up from the old house, he would place it in the exact same spot, correspondingly, in the new one. What did that mean? What was he thinking? What did he think about her? Did he still love her? Had he ever, really?

Trying to see into somebody . . . trying to see what

the truth was . . . Sometimes Maureen didn't think there was any truth, or if there was, each person had his own, dark and murky, like the roads and houses and lives deep, deep under the waters of Truman Reservoir.

*

When she got back to the house, Johnny's pickup was gone, but the bathtub sat in the middle of the kitchen, two long black gashes in the linoleum between it and the door. She found George lying on his side on his bed, mouth open, saliva forming a dark circle on the quilt. She caught her breath, thinking he was dead, but then his eyes moved.

Ella must have returned with George, then left for Sedalia. It was just as well. Maureen was in no mood for small talk. Besides, the ice cream had melted in the back seat of the car while she sat mooning by the water.

George's eyes searched around the room, landed on nothing.

"The lilacs . . ." he said, voice thin and scratchy. "The shade . . ."

"It's the grove, isn't it, George? You'd like to see the grove again."

"We lie in the shade."

She stroked his hair, pulled him up to a sitting position, hugged him.

Where was Johnny? Ella wouldn't have left him there by himself. Would Johnny? Would he leave his own father?

Suddenly, Maureen pulled George up to his feet.

"Come on, George. Do you want to see your grove

again? You'd like to see your grove again, wouldn't you?"

She led George out of the house, across the yard past the barn and machine shed and through the gate into the pasture. The few head of cattle that Johnny still kept were down at the bottom of the hill in the shade of the trees by the creek.

She led George on up to the knoll of the hill.

"Wasn't this it, George? Isn't this where the grove was?"

" ... lilacs ..."

Yes, right there at their feet was a stump cut level with the ground, almost a foot across. Yes, over there was another.

"Sit with me in the shade of the grove, George."

She managed to get him down on his hands and knees, then sort of rolled him around until he was sitting, legs stretched out straight in front of him. She sat beside him with her legs crossed, arm around his waist so he wouldn't fall back.

"What was here, George, maple trees?"

George looked up into the sky, frowned.

"Yes, here is one, George. See it? And look at this one over here. I didn't realize maples got so tall. Look how the leaves are turning, George. How bright the reds are!"

"Lilacs," George muttered, staring up at the sky.

"Yes, so beautiful. When they first begin to leaf out like this is when lilacs smell the sweetest, isn't that true, George? How sweet—you can almost taste it."

She could almost taste it. It was sweet spring among the lilacs, a crisp fall under the maples. She put a maple here, here, here, hung a sweet curtain of lilacs between those two over there.

"... lilacs ..."

All that remained for George, all from his long
life— lilacs and maples, a picnic with Opal in the grove.
All that remained. ... Maureen envied him so fiercely she
wanted to shout, to weep. What would remain for her?

"... lilacs ..."

Another maple tree, another one here, now a lilac
bush, a canopy of lilacs, sweet under the spring sky, the
cool fall sky. Maples and lilacs all around, so thick she
could no longer see the house, the cornfield beyond. If
Johnny were to drive up in his pickup now from the
Workman place, she wouldn't have to see, wouldn't be
able to see what he'd brought this time, and he wouldn't
see them either, would he? And yet, and yet, she heard
the pickup stop beside the house, heard him walking
through the gate, across the pasture toward the grove,
heard him wind his way surely and swiftly through the
lilacs and maples until he found them there, Johnny with
his sweet smile, and he held it out to her, Maureen, what
he'd taken from George's house, a mirror with a beautiful
gilt frame that she'd not seen before but which must have
come from George and Opal's bedroom. He held the mir-
ror toward her and she said, Is this for me? and he said,
Of course it's for you, everything has been for you, didn't
you realize that? and she said, Why, though, why? and he
said, Because I love you. And she looked into the mirror—
lovely, lovely—and knew that what he said must be true.

*

She smelled it, more than just urine this time. She
helped George to his feet. His pants were caked with

mud—dust and urine—and his face, wet with sweat, glowed a ghostly white in the fierce sun. He trembled in the heat and looked frightened.

"Oh George, George, what have I done?"

"Lilacs," he said.

She held him, looked around the dusty field, round faces of the tree stumps staring dumbly up at her.

"George, George, what can we do when the years go by so, and there's so little left? How can we live?"

*

She protects him from the cold water with her body. With her hands she spreads out her long thick brown hair like a Japanese fan to catch the spray. With her own hands—no cloth—she lathers up the soap and washes him, face, neck, shoulders, arms, hands. As she kneels to wash his legs and feet, the water, warm now, falls down on her like a spring shower. When she washes his privates, his penis hangs down longer and longer as if pointing to something below the ground. She wonders if he's remembering something then. She would settle for what he remembers, whatever it is.

As she washes and rinses, she massages his loose, rubbery flesh, the slack muscle—ghost of muscle—beneath. George likes this. He leans against her and purrs. When he grows cold—and he always grows cold—she presses him to her, holds him like a great, fragile, dear thing.

"Opal," he whispers, smiling down at her.

"Yes," she nods, "Opal."

PASSOVER

1.

"PROBLEMS?"

Nurse Houten, a choleric veteran of three decades of rural health service wars, eyed Dr. Fine dourly a moment before answering.

"Anything different about tonight?" she said finally. "Another night, another problem. Better talk to Chester. He's the one who said to call you. In the snack bar."

As he headed off down the east wing of the clinic toward the staff snack bar, Dr. Fine let out a long, loud sigh. But except for a few patients in their rooms behind closed doors, there was no one to appreciate it. It was Easter weekend, and half of the staff had been given Saturday off. Tomorrow, only essential staff would be on hand. Still, someone had thought fit to call *him* in—not only his day off, but Passover beginning in a couple of hours. Would these hillbilly Baptists think of that, though? What a joke.

But, although he was trying hard to work up a bad mood, he had to admit that he wasn't all that bothered. His family was half a continent away in New York, there was no Jewish community in Clinton, the nearest temple was an hour's drive away in Sedalia, and, hell, he hadn't observed the Holy Days for years anyway. Frankly, he was grateful for something to do.

He found Chester Barns sitting at a table and staring morosely into a cup of coffee. Hungover again, Dr. Fine guessed.

Chester glanced up, then back down at the coffee. "Ben."

Chester Barns watched *St. Elsewhere* regularly and fancied himself cut from the same cloth as the witty, confident black orderly, Luther. But Chester was more surly than assertive, and he angered the hospital administrator and most of the physicians by calling them by their first names. Still, he worked capably and sensitively with the patients—when he was sober—and was open and friendly once he warmed to a person and shed the Luther routine, and Ben had soon grown to like him.

"What's up, Chester?"

"Mary Carter's gone," he said.

"My God! Mary Carter, dead?"

Ben was surprised by a sudden stab of grief, more surprised when his mother's face appeared to him, a gentle but gaunt and vaguely accusing death mask. "She's gone," his father had wailed over the phone, long distance from New York, "my Ruthie. She was sitting at the breakfast table, her head went back. By the time I got around the table, she was gone. Pray for the dead, Benny."

"Hell no," Chester said, "not dead, gone.Walked. Vamoosed. Took her coat and purse, but the rest of her clothes and suitcase, they're still here."

Ben frowned and canted his head toward Chester as if he hadn't heard him quite clearly.

Old Mary Carter, who for two weeks hadn't been able to get out of bed without help, had simply walked away? He couldn't believe it. They'd brought her in on a stretcher over two weeks ago. The mailman had seen her through the window in her front door, lying on the floor.

"Any idea what's wrong with her?" Ben had asked the ambulance attendant who'd wheeled her in, and Mary had rolled her head over toward him and said, "I just got wore out."

"Wore out from living," the attendant had clucked sympathetically.

"No, wore out from *walking*," Mary had said.

She would not talk, except to Ben. He would check in on her daily, even on his days off, and they would chat. She seemed to enjoy it, even though her talk was mostly a bitter lament.

She had moved to Clinton a decade ago from a little backwater on the edge of the Ozarks called Sunday's Hollow, no more than ten or fifteen miles from Clinton, but a whole different world to her. Then why had she come if it was such a change?

"I didn't know what it'd be like, did I?" she'd said, voice rising. Behind the rheumy eyes, blue-veined temples, and wasted body Ben could occasionally detect something iron, easily brought to anger.

"I didn't know what I was getting into. Besides, I'd lived alone for five years after my husband died, down in that hollow, all alone. I thought I could make a go of it for a while, but when I got to talking to the squirrels, I figured it was time to move out. Thought with all the people in a city a body couldn't get lonely, but I was wrong about that, too. Well, it didn't make a whole lot of difference why I came or where I went. It was just a matter of time before I'd've had to leave the hollow anyway."

She'd sold the farm to land developers who figured to divide it into lots and build cottages on them, sell them as summer homes to people from Kansas City once the Harry S Truman dam was finished. She'd never gone back, but she'd heard that something fell through—they'd never built the cottages, but they'd knocked her house down anyway, and the waters from the dam had backed up through the hollow, forming a major arm of the Harry S Truman Reservoir. The water, she'd been told, had come up to within thirty feet of where the house had stood.

"So here I was, stuck. I didn't know anybody, didn't know how to do anything. Didn't know how to pay my taxes, didn't know how to go about finding a doctor, didn't know how to take care of the car. So I sold the car and took a cab if I had to go someplace. Then I got to worrying about how awful much the cab cost, how much the groceries cost. I stopped going out, bought only enough food to keep me alive, didn't see much point to that even. I worried about everything, worried about worrying. I'd get up at three in the morning and walk, in the house, just walk and walk. I'd walk all day until I couldn't stand up no more. Guess I forgot to eat. I keeled over. The mailman found me, or I'd still be there. Bad break for the rats. I should've stayed home. Should have stayed home in the hollow, faced it there. If I could get back ..."

"Home," Ben said, breaking out of his reverie. "She went home."

"Nope. Police checked there first thing yesterday. Checked all around between here and her house."

"Yesterday!"

"Yep. She took off sometime between lunch and when they brought her medicine around in the middle of the afternoon."

"Jesus. Why didn't anybody call me before this?"

"Didn't think of it, I guess. I didn't know about it either until I came on duty today. I was the one suggested they try you. Figured you knew her better than anyone else around here."

It was true. Mary Carter had taken to Ben, in some way seemed to sense a kinship with him, although he didn't know why.

"Chester, did Mary ever talk to you about that place out in the sticks that she came from? Sunday's Hollow, over close to Warsaw, I think."

"Nope. Me and her didn't talk much."

"That's all she ever talked about, how she was sorry she had moved to Clinton. Do you think she might've tried to go back there?"

"Well, maybe. Person can *try* anything. But trying ain't doing. Come to think of it, though, she was a walker, wasn't she? Ain't that what got her here in the first place?"

Ben looked at his watch. Suddenly, the fact of frail

old Mary Carter wandering alone for over twenty-four hours swept over him like a raw March wind.

He headed for the door.

"I'm going to look for Mary Carter. Want to come?"

"Naw, I'm working, remember?" Chester said, squeezing his head between his hands and grimacing.

Ben returned to the reception desk. He decided it might be a good idea to call the police to see if they'd turned up anything. But no, they had no news about Mary. They'd had two patrol cars out looking for her all yesterday afternoon, had talked to people living along the streets leading away from the hospital, and had inquired at the taxi company, but no one had seen her. They'd had to call off the search during the night because of the fire at the lumber yard on the edge of town.

Ben recalled seeing a smudge of smoke on the eastern horizon this morning when he had gone out to get the paper.

He hung up and headed for the door, where he bumped into Chester, who was coming back in with a paper bag in his hand.

"You really thinking about heading out into the boonies, late as it's getting?"

Ben looked out and saw that it was nearly dark.

"Yeh," he nodded, growing impatient. Mary'd been out there a whole night and a day already, and another night coming on.

Chester frowned skeptically.

"You ate?"

Ben shook his head.

"Here, then, take this," Chester said, pushing the bag toward Ben. "After all I been drinking, my stomach just sort of takes to its heels at the thought of solid food."

Ben now was in too big a hurry even for polite refusals. He took the bag, thanked Chester, and headed for the parking lot. In his car he opened the bag and found some soda crackers, a hardboiled egg, and a ham sandwich.

"Ham sandwich! These goyim," Ben sighed, tossing the bag down on the seat.

"Observe the High Holy Days, that much at least, Benny," had been the last thing that his mother had said to him when he left New York to begin his family practice residency at the University of Missouri School of Medicine. From there he had come to Clinton, on the edge of the Ozarks, to work at the Henry County Regional Health Clinic.

Although to others his mother's request might have seemed natural enough, it came as a shock to Ben. She had never had much to say about religion, never had much to say about anything, in fact. When Ben thought of his mother, he thought of a small, dark woman who suffered her husband's mercurial swings of mood in stoical if bemused patience. Until she made that request, it had never occurred to Ben that her patience might have had some basis in faith. Even then, he wasn't sure. He never knew how things stood, in reference to religion, in his own home.

"Observe the High Holy Days, that much at least, Benny, for me," she had said.

He could remember no other request that she had ever made of him. Except once, when he announced that he was applying to medical school, she had sighed, with a curious smile on her face, "I had always hoped that you'd become a rabbi." Ben thought she was joking, a dig at his father, but he wasn't sure if his father would think it funny or not. With his father he was never sure what to expect.

Ben had pulled out of the parking lot and had reached the four-way stop at the next corner before he realized that he didn't know where he was going. Sunday's Hollow was east somewhere; that's all he knew. Then the silliness of the whole undertaking hit him. Why drive to Sunday's Hollow when Mary Carter couldn't possibly have walked that far? She would have known that as well as anyone. She was old, tired, bitter—but not crazy.

And yet—home. There it was. That was all she'd talked about, down in that hollow. And not always fondly, either. It'd been a hard life, hard work, little money. Rural poverty, that's what it amounted to—just what Ben had come to Missouri to find. Hadn't it been visions of the rural poor that kindled an almost embarrassing but not to be denied missionary zeal in Ben? And he had set their broken bones and treated their fevers and, sometimes, eased as best he could their dying. In return, he'd received neither gratitude nor intimacy. The waiting room was still always full, and they were still always poor and faceless. But what had he expected?

"You want poor, go to Bedford-Stuy," his father had said. "Stay home, Benny. Stay among your own people."

Your own people! Ben couldn't believe his ears. He could think of nothing to say in reply because he couldn't imagine what had motivated his father to say such a thing, couldn't imagine what he was thinking. But then he never understood his father, so he tossed away the request like one more stone into the sea of the unfathomable.

"Why do you want to go home?" he had asked Mary. She was stooped and gnarled from the work, hard all her life but harder yet after her husband died.

Her husband was an Indian fellow, Ben seemed to recall. Some Indian name.

"Home is where you lived, where your life was, that's all. You go away from home, you're going away from your own life. You're lost. Oh, I don't know. I can't explain it. But I want to go back, even if there's nothing there."

Often, at some point when she was talking about home, she would try to raise herself up on the bed to look out the window, where a redbud tree grew. Sometimes Ben would have to help her.

"I'd like to be home to see the redbuds bloom one more time," she'd say. "We were married in the spring, and when he brought me home to his cabin, there was a wreath of redbud blooms on the door. He'd made it with his own hands. I knew then that I'd married a gentle man."

Ben would be taken aback when Mary fell into one of her more wistfully lyrical moments. Mostly she was a somber woman, not quite bitter, not quite cynical, but close to both, especially when she spoke of the loneliness of being married to an Indian.

Robin's Song Carter! That was his name, Ben suddenly remembered. Robin's Song's father—another bird name, Eagle? Blackbird? Mockingbird! yes, Mockingbird—had sold his farm to Mary's father when Mary's family moved into Sunday's Hollow from Pennsylvania. Most of the Osage Indians were moving out of the hollow by then, but instead of leaving, the Carters bought another farm up on the hill. That was where Mary and Robin's Song lived. By then, there were only a few Osage families left in the area—the Carters, the Wallens, and . . . Ben couldn't remember the other names. It'd been hard married to an Indian. An Indian wasn't quite a white man, and a white woman married to an Indian was, well, a puzzle. She'd come to feel like a stranger in her own country. That was one reason the decision to move to Clinton hadn't seemed such a hard one. Only after she was there and began to worry did she see that the hollow had been home, her life, and leaving a mistake.

"Stranger in a strange land, that's what I felt like in Clinton. I'd never lived in a city, you see."

Ben had almost laughed. A city! He tried to picture Mary in Belle Harbor. From his father's house on Newport they could walk to Jamaica Bay in two minutes. He'd show her the skyline of Manhattan, seeming to rise right up out of the water, across the Bay. Clinton, a city?

But he didn't laugh. He understood. He also was a stranger in Clinton, and he too had been a stranger in his own land. Worse, a stranger in his own house.

Ben found himself on the edge of Clinton. A 7-Eleven store was on the right, and he pulled in and filled up the car with gasoline.

The attendant, a man in a plaid shirt with a half-dozen ballpoint pens and a tire gauge sticking up out of his shirt pocket, seemed in a talking mood, so for the hell of it Ben described Mary Carter and asked if he might have seen her sometime. The man remembered her right away.

"She come walking up from this way," he said, pointing back to the west, "and went walking off that way," pointing off to the east. "She kind of slowed down when she got across from the store like she might be coming in, but then she just went on. Thought it was mighty odd at the time. What's it all about?"

Ben began to tell the old fellow about Mary, a little impatiently, though—he was in a hurry now—and a little apologetically, as if his theory about Mary trying to get home were too farfetched to be taken seriously.

"Walking home!" The man smiled sadly and ran a hand through his hair. "Isn't that something? I'll tell you, though, you can't ever tell what a person will accomplish, they set their mind to it. . . . So, you doctor down at the clinic? My sister was in there with kidney trouble a while back. Treated her real nice. Name of Bessie Scroggs. Maybe you remember her."

Ben didn't.

"And you are doctor who?"

"Fine. Benjamin Fine."

"Oh, Jewish fella."

Ben felt himself bristling, his jaw clenching.

"God's chosen. Chosen people of God."

The old man said it kindly and sincerely, and Ben was strangely moved. He didn't know what to say. He waved vaguely and went out to his car.

God's chosen! He didn't know whether to laugh or cry. His father would laugh, that was for sure. For sure? When was he ever sure about his father?

He couldn't think of his father without also thinking of a dimmer figure, looking stern, almost forbidding, in a long black coat and black hat, the hair curling over his ears—but kind, his voice gentle, loving. His grandfather, Samuel, who would take him up into the finished attic over the house on Newport when Ben was four, five, and read to him from a huge book, his eyes shining with what Ben would later realize was profound faith, the voice loving but in his excitement always threatening to rise far above the self-imposed whisper. Remember all of this, Benny, he would say. And then the strange but somehow comforting teachings. What to eat, what not, what to put on your right, what to put away from you. Ben strained to remember, but could not.

Always, his father would find them and take Ben by the hand and lead him away from Samuel. Never in anger, though. His father would be troubled, would take Ben on his lap, preparing to speak, but often as not he would only stare off into space and say nothing.

His father sent him to the public grammar school in Rockaway, but then old Samuel died when Ben was ready for the fourth grade, and, without explanation, his father enrolled him in the Yeshiva of Belle Harbor.

At the Yeshiva, Ben often thought of his fellow students as Jews and himself as something other than a Jew.

His father would go for months and not say a word about religion, or if he mentioned it at all it was only to mock the Jews. Then, for no apparent reason, on some High Holy Day he would enact strange rites, his face streaming with tears.

His mother was always in the background, patiently enduring. Ben knew that she went to temple regularly, but she never spoke to him concerning his faith—or lack of it.

After all that—that history of nothing—a rare bolt from the blue. From his mother: First, "I had always hoped that you'd become a rabbi." Then, "Observe the High Holy Days, at least that, Benny." And his father: "Stay home. Stay among your own people." What was he supposed to have made of it all?

Damn, here he was again, daydreaming when he should be off looking for Mary. But look where? She'd walked off somewhere into the night, but if she had collapsed along the road—the most likely possibility—surely someone would have seen her come daylight.

Ben took the road map of Missouri out of the glove compartment. Highway 7 meandered between Clinton and Warsaw, but there was no notation for Sunday's Hollow.

He was, in fact, on Highway 7. Taking that for a sign, he started up the car and headed east.

2.

He was lost, God was he lost.

Highway 7 had twisted, turned, dipped, climbed over, around, and beneath hills for what seemed like half the night, until Ben found himself on the edge of Warsaw. He had somehow gone past Sunday's Hollow.

He stopped at a Phillips 66 station and asked directions. The attendant, a young man, probably a high school kid working at night, had heard of Sunday's

Hollow, he thought, but wasn't sure.

"Ain't it off west some place? Well, you might oughta taken 13 south out of Clinton, then cut over on 52 at Deepwater."

That would've taken Ben south of the long arm of Truman Reservoir that stretched between Warsaw and Clinton. Seven took him north of the arm.

The attendant thought there was a road that cut across the arm, over a bridge, a left a few miles out of Warsaw. He didn't know the number. If Ben could hit that road, it'd take him over the water. Otherwise, he'd have to go all the way back to Clinton and start over.

Ben drove back west on Highway 7, slowly, looking for the road. He found a blacktop cutting off to the left. It seemed awfully narrow and had no sign on it, but Ben took it anyway. He drove and drove, decided this couldn't be the road, turned around and drove and drove and drove. Why hadn't he come to 7? He stopped, turned around, and drove some more.

He was lost. He pulled into a gravel road—more of a wide path—leading off the blacktop and shut off the engine. There was no use driving anymore in the dark. He settled back against the seat, closed his eyes. It was too cold to sleep, he thought.

He awoke to see a face staring down at him through the windshield. The man was tapping on the glass.

"We're about ready to begin," the man said.

Ben reared, tried to shake the sleep out of his head.

Other cars lined the dirt road ahead of him, and to his right a field rose to a small, bare hill upon which dozens of men, women, and children stood or sat on blankets and aluminum lawn chairs. Dawn was just breaking, and the light seemed to slant upward toward the people on the hill.

"We're ready to begin," the man said again.

Ben rolled down the window.

"Begin what?"

"Why, Easter sunrise service. Isn't that why you're here?"

"No," he said, embarrassed and confused. It took him a moment to remember why he was there. "No, I'm looking for a woman. Mary Carter."

"Old Mary Carter, you mean? The widow woman? She moved off years ago. She's in Clinton now."

Ben brightened.

"Oh, you know of the Carters, then?"

The man identified himself as Reverend Asa Greene, the minister of the Calvary Baptist Church, just down the road—Ben couldn't have missed it. And, yes, he knew the Carters. His grandfather and then his father had been the minister at the New Hope Baptist Church until it was destroyed to make way for the reservoir that filled Sunday's Hollow, and he, the father, had been lifelong friends with Mary's brother, George Workman. George was dead now and Mary had moved on to Clinton after selling the old Carter place.

"You won't find her here, I'm afraid."

Ben explained his mission.

With an expression of sadness, alarm, and something like amusement, the Reverend shook his head.

"Walk all this way? Doc, the people that grow up around here are as tough as shoe leather, most of them, but a wore out old woman just ain't gonna walk fifteen miles. But sure, I can tell you how to get to the Carter place if you want to take a look. It's only a couple of miles. But there's not much left."

Ben said he'd take a look anyway.

Because the road was so choked by weeds and washed out by erosion, Ben had had to abandon the car fifty yards from the house, or what had once been the house. Now there was only a rectangular block of concrete—the foundation— looking absurdly small in the middle of what had once been the yard. On top of the concrete slab was a rocking chair, and sitting in the rocking chair, her head tilted back at an awkward angle, was Mary Carter. Ben knew she was dead the moment he saw her.

He scrambled up on the block, which was elevated about four feet above the level of the ground, and stared at Mary.

How had she gotten here? She couldn't have walked all this way, it was impossible. Did she hitch a ride? The vision of frail old Mary Carter standing on the side of the road with her thumb out struck Ben as so ludicrous that he could have laughed.

But he did not laugh. Once more he thought of his mother. He had not mourned at her funeral. On the flight back from Missouri, at the funeral, and during the short stay afterward with his father, he had felt vaguely disoriented. But he had not mourned.

Bile, dark and bitter, rose in his throat.

Ben could not bear to look at Mary. He turned away, and in turning saw stretching off toward the sun the waters of the lake, not thirty feet below.

The sun was now fully up, and the water blazed with golds and fiery reds, glowing purples floating in pools of silver. There were redbuds bordering the water, just beginning to leaf out, and a few were covered with tiny pink blossoms.

It was the waters that Mary had last seen, she was facing the waters, where Sunday's Hollow once was. And maybe she thought, maybe she died thinking, how beautiful it all is! Maybe she had died happy. It was possible, wasn't it? Maybe she had died thanking God for this one last sight.

Or had she died frozen to the chair in the dark of night, terrified, despairing, and alone?

Ben heaped dirt on her. He heaped dirt on her.

Ben found his way back to the hill where the sunrise service was.

He heard them singing as he drove up. He got out of the car and slouched back against the side, prepared to wait. But almost immediately Reverend Greene started over toward him. Ben made a gesture motioning him back, but he came on.

"My part's over anyway," the Reverend said. "They're just filled with the Lord and singing for joy. They'll be here awhile yet."

Ben told him about finding Mary Carter.

"In a rocking chair! Now where do you think that came from?"

The question hadn't occurred to Ben, and he was a little irritated that it seemed to be all that interested Reverend Greene.

The singing rang through the bright air.

Oh Lamb of God, I come,
I come.

Ben was struck by the absurd wonder of it all. Here he was, Benjamin Fine of Belle Harbor, New York, grandson of black-hatted Samuel Fine, standing on a hillside in the Missouri Ozarks listening to goyim singing Easter hymns. And he had missed the first night of Passover!

He shook his head bitterly.

Reverend Greene reached over and patted him on the shoulder.

"You did your best, young man. We'll go over and take care of things after I finish up here. Now, no sense grieving for Mary Carter. And why should we, when you think about it? I mean, after all, she made it, didn't she? She wanted to come home, and she came home. That's a triumph of some sort, isn't it? Maybe we should rejoice."

Maybe. Ben wasn't sure, but, yes, maybe.

The only thing that he was certain of was that it had been a long night and already a long day, filled, he somehow felt, with portents, meanings. But portending, meaning, what exactly?

Ben wished the signs were easier to read.

He made himself a promise, though, that when he got back to Clinton, he would light a candle, if he had one, and, if he could remember them, he would say prayers for the dead.